PRAISE FOR "SPLIT SCREAM VOLUME THREE"

"Two confrontations with the fleshy, dripping excesses of expression, the urges burbling up and out of Barb and McCarthy's characters onto the page and over the margins. Bodies as tragic exhibitions only these authors can name."

—Andrew F. Sullivan, author of *The Marigold* and *The Handyman Method*

"Reading the stories in the Volume Three made me think this just might be the perfect length for horror fiction. [They] are a real kick in the head, combining the urgency of the short form with the characterization, texture, and nuance of longer works. Both authors deserve recognition for the maturity and ingenuity of their writing.

Both tales are told with admirable skill, with attention to pacing and characterization as well as shock value. Although you can read the entire volume in one evening, you will end with a sense of having taken a much longer journey."

— S.P. Miskowski, author of *I Wish I Was Like You*

"SPLIT SCREAM Volume Three offers up a strong publication with stories by Patrick Barb and J.A.W. McCarthy. With threads of twisted secrets and a worship of art, both tales successfully create in-depth worlds where darkness lingers. Barb's character-driven, cosmic tale steadily builds up unique layers for readers to discover as a deeper truth is constructed, which balances nicely with McCarthy's lush prose where layers are bled away in a beautifully poetic and visceral story. Does art heal or destroy the characters within both tales? Readers will have to pick up this delightful pairing to find out!"

—Sara Tantlinger, Bram Stoker Award-winning author of *The Devil's Dreamland*

"The third volume of the SPLIT SCREAM series features its most cohesive pairing yet. Barb's and McCarthy's stories reflect and refract. Both are deeply enamored with art, while exploring vastly different pathological vistas. The result is a duo that compliments each other's aesthetics in one highly readable volume, covering both weirded-out slashers and neo-gothic tragedy."

—Carson Winter, author of Soft Targets

PRAISE FOR "SO QUIET, SO WHITE" by PATRICK BARB

"'So Quiet, So White' is an edgy, suspenseful tale of paranoia, set in a remote small town where locals blame a teenager for a recent massacre. The teen's grandfather, Roger Grimsby, is an artist known primarily for his gruesome paperback covers, and his recollections hint at secret pacts and bloody sacrifices beyond the present crisis. Barb has created such an intense, hallucinogenic atmosphere around this isolated community, the imagery and the setting will stay with you for a long time."

—S.P. Miskowski, author of I Wish I Was Like You

PRAISE FOR "IMAGO EXPULSIO (THE RED ANIMAL OF OUR BLOOD)" by J.A.W. McCARTHY

"'Imago Expulsio (The Red Animal of Our Blood)' offers an impressive visceral combination of cosmic horror and body horror in a tale of two artists. The erotic becomes inextricably entwined with something terribly sinister, as we follow the protagonist's desperate attempts to save her beloved. McCarthy's success at devising a moving, plausible love story within this struggle demonstrates exceptional artistry."

— S.P. Miskowski, author of I Wish I Was Like You

SPLIT SCREAM

Volume Three

Featuring:

Patrick Barb

&

J.A.W. McCarthy

Published by Tenebrous Press.
Visit our website at www.tenebrouspress.com.

First Tenebrous Printing, November 2023.

Originally printed by Dread Stone Press, July 2023.

Print ISBN: 978-1-959790-17-4
eBook ISBN: 978-1-959790-18-1

Cover illustrations by Evangeline Gallagher.

Interior illustrations by Ryan Mills.

Cover and interior design by Dreadful Designs.

Edited by Alex Ebenstein.

For the ones sticking with us.

INTRODUCTION

T he novelette has been dismissed and disparaged. Some dictionaries don't even define them as a unique form, listing only short stories, novellas, or novels. Others write them off as being "too sentimental" or "trivial".

This is silly, of course, and, with little effort it's easy to see the novelette has a purpose and value.

What makes a novelette, then? Exact word counts vary, but these stories are longer than a short story and shorter than a novella. In this case, between ten and twenty thousand words; or, horror you can devour in about an hour or two.

Sound like another form of storytelling?

I'm not saying a novelette is a movie is a novelette. And I'm not saying written fiction *needs* to be like movies. But… But they are *kind of* like movies in terms of length and threads, right? If you're willing to accept that premise, at least for the moment, may I present to you…

SPLIT SCREAM
A Novelette Double Feature

Truly, what better way to present these stories than as a double feature? Do you *have* to read them back to back in a single Friday night after dusk? Certainly not. But could you? Absolutely.

Shall we?

Our first stop is the Grimsby House in and amongst the towering pines. It's Patrick Barb's "So Quiet, So White," where a man and his grandson demonstrate the balancing act of creative arts and destructive forces. Then, in another house, a vomiting painting sits atop the mantle. But what can that painting, and J.A.W. McCarthy's "Imago Expulsio (The Red Animal of Our Blood)," tell us about love and devotion? A vow is made, but where's the line? Nonexistent? Let's find out.

Okay. Are you ready? Grab some popcorn, turn the lights low, and don't be afraid to scream.

This is a second printing for Volume Three of the SPLIT SCREAM series, now in its new home at Tenebrous Press. If you're new to the series, welcome! If you've read any prior volume or iteration, my heartfelt thanks to you for coming back. In any case, I do hope you enjoy, and that you seek out more.

Long live the novelette!

Alex Ebenstein
Tenebrous Press
Michigan, USA
October 2023

CONTENTS

SO QUIET, SO WHITE

Patrick Barb

Twin beams of pale light pierce the darkness, illuminating the front façade of the old backwoods country house that locals call *the Grimsby House*. The vehicle's headlights resemble the eyes of a nocturnal scavenger sneaking up as close as it dares to civilization so it can dig through the refuse for the tastiest morsels. The abrupt appearance of this light outside his home doesn't wake Roger because he's not gone to bed yet. As it stands, he's been sleeping less and less since they released his grandson from the hospital and let the boy return to his grandfather's care. That permission came with gruff warnings to both that they "shouldn't leave town." Roger Grimsby, who gave his name to the Grimsby House, isn't one to dwell on those types of threats though. He's well aware of his and his grandson's rights and the words of a sheriff twenty years his junior won't be the thing to cause him a sleepless night.

Most evenings, Roger's upstairs in his studio working on that week's painting commissions, keeping one or two canvases ahead of the next deadline. Lost in the brushwork for a retro creature-feature piece, adding details of radioactive crackle beneath the buzz and hum of his many work lamps. He keeps the overhead lights on as well. He's awash in their electric glow, leaving the darkness to its own designs.

As a result of this cocooning in artificial light, it takes a moment for the extra bit of illumination outside to register for Roger.

Something pops in his back when he straightens. His doctor's monthly matter-of-fact recitation of everything Roger does wrong in his day-to-day existence plays on a loop in his head. "You need more sleep, don't sit like that, you need to exercise, don't worry so much…"

Roger slides his feet into the house shoes he keeps nearby and the old wood floor creaks under his slow trudge around the room. He turns off the lamps and flips the switch for the overheads. Darkness falls with slick determination, like a damp bath towel slithering off a towel rack and unfurling across a steamed-up bathroom floor. Living on a mill road with an acre of towering pines with spindly branches exploding toward the sky on either side, separating his home from the nearest neighbor and the rest of the world, when the lights go off in Roger's home no star shine or moonglow's getting in.

But those twin beams remain steady in their silent assessment of the house.

It's Clint. Gotta be. Boy snuck out, now he's pushing the old Mustang down the drive so I won't hear when he cranks that engine. It's what his daddy used to do. Too bad Clint probably snuck into my stash beforehand and got himself too shitfaced pre-gaming on my Johnny Walker to notice he'd gone and turned the high beams on...

Clint's *daddy* was Roger's son though. Richie.

Richie: the lost and broken link in a chain meant to connect the old artist and the sullen teen now living under the roof of the Grimsby House. Back when Richie was the one trying to creep out or back home (depending on the hour), Roger had the bandwidth to work on his paint-ings—cranking them out to keep up with the demand of paperback publishers whose lurid horror titles filled the racks of the grocery marts until they didn't—*and* to listen for his son's foolhardy attempts at sneaking around in a too-loud and too-fast car.

Now, when he's lost in his work and the quiet leaves him holding conversations in his head to pass the time, Roger's certain he wouldn't even notice if Clint pulled out, Mustang's tires spinning gravel, horn honking loud enough to wake the Brandons' coon dogs next door.

In the dark, his hands grip the window. Arms tensed, he's prepared to push it open and give this intruder more than a little piece of his mind.

But he stops short of doing so. Instead, he steps away from the latch and stands in the shaft of light bouncing up from the slick gray stones of the gravel driveway. Gazing out the window, Roger spots his silhouette etched across the ground, a black form in the middle of a white circle. Like the Man in the Moon's crash-landed in the front yard.

Moon and all.

Roger waits. And listens.

Listens and waits.

He's sure the Mustang's engine growls in the dark, like a caged lion whose lazy afternoon at the zoo's been interrupted by someone falling over the protective barrier surrounding the beast's enclosure. An unexpected treat to reveal the limits of the savage creature's domestication…

No matter how far they come, it's never far enough.

Then, Roger changes his mind about what's rumbling, deciding it's much closer. Now, he's sure it's his stomach making the racket. He believes he ate *some meal* that day. But he's not certain. Things like food get away from him when he's painting.

"Grandpa! A car's in the driveway! I dunno whose."

With the exclamation from the downstairs bedroom that Clint's staked for his own and inhabited ever since the boy's daddy *went away*, Roger's breath hitches. It's like he's taken a bad swallow of rotten moonshine reality. The truth goes down the wrong tube and it burns.

"Shit."

Downstairs, Clint's plodding teenage feet stomp toward the front of the house, echoing with each step so it sounds like he's an army of one. "Gonna check who it is out…" The boy's grumbling speech lapses into incoherent muttering.

Probably believing he's still asleep and this is all some strange dream, right?

Roger doesn't fault him for that mistaken perception. After all, it's been a while since any visitors pulled up their winding driveway.

Only one bar way out this way, the Miller's Daughter. Is that ol' juke-joint even still open?

When Richie was a kid, the family would get drunks pulling off the mill road and onto their driveway, slow-rolling the vehicles close enough to the Grimsby House—but never *too close*. They'd sleep off their drunk and be gone by morning. Harmless.

Hell, it was a sure sight better for public safety than having 'em driving drunk and too fast on these old country roads out here.

But another voice, striving to make itself heard from the back of Roger's head, suggests there's something more at play. It's a familiar voice, but one he hasn't heard from in years. Suddenly, it finds its tone and tenor once again, before proceeding to tell the old man that the person behind the wheel carries ill intentions directed at the old house's two inhabitants.

Roger doesn't have his number listed and he keeps his address out of the phone book white pages as well. Since he uses a P.O. box for his art business, he doesn't find much reason for folks to know where precisely he hangs his hat.

Still, they live in a small town. Small enough for someone to procure that information quite easily if it's what they desire. God knows the reporters had dug the details up fast enough after the news about the dead bodies at Clint's summer camp broke onto the national wires. Cars and vans parked in crooked lines on either side of the old mill road, all their tires sinking into the churned-up muddy roadside. Heavy cameras hefted on wide shoulders swept across the pines until they found a gap in the foliage, then they waited for Roger's truck to emerge from the driveway and turn onto the road. Those savvy camera operators snapped photo after photo in a blur of hot, white light. He couldn't see their faces then, but he could well imagine what they looked like. Eager, desperate, hungry.

Now, Roger can't help but wonder: *did all those cars and trucks and vans belong to professionals, folks out doing a job and looking for a good story? Or a good angle on a bad story? Behind the flashes, the ebony camera shutters' blinking, was someone else blending in with the crowd and watching us? Waiting?*

Staring into the night, those thoughts thrive like mushrooms. They soon fill every available space in his head with a meaty-sweet sickness.

"Don't…" Roger's warning starts well enough, but falls apart when he begins to move. As his legs start to get away from him, he wobbles at the top of the stairs, gripping the wooden banister so hard he'll be picking splinters out of his palm until sunrise. By the time he's recovered and finished his warning, it comes out as a weak, watery croak. "…open that door. Don't!"

Light shines through the front of the house into the first floor, so when Clint turns to face his grandfather the backlighting hides his face in shadows. As though all the darkness outside has concentrated in the foyer and then got itself dressed up in the teenager's hand-me-down Lynyrd Skynyrd t-shirt and boxer shorts—the raggedy pair with hearts on them.

"Grandpa?"

"Go back to bed," Roger says, finding his voice once more.

"But…"

"Whoever it is, they'll leave soon enough. If they wanted something, they'd let us know."

The boy grumbles, but it's less from frustration at his grandpa and more from being disturbed from whatever pursuits teenage boys get up to in their rooms when they'd probably be better off just sleeping. In the end, he listens though. By the time Roger's made it down the stairs, he's the only one still up and about in the house.

And that's just fine as far as he's concerned.

Time passes.

When the sun finally comes through the front windows, dark circles ring Roger's bloodshot eyes. His back and knees ache even more from sitting up all night, staring at the high beams until they departed, taking the car and the driver with them. He'd spent the rest of his time staring into the void of the night remaining. *In case they come back.* Black spots encased in corpse-pale white explode behind his eyes until he adds a couple fingers of bourbon to his Folger's—all of the black liquid poured into an old spiderweb-cracked mug declaring Roger to be the "World's Greatest Grandpa."

The downstairs telephone rings. Roger answers, but waits for the person on the other end of the line to speak first.

"Mr. Grimsby?"

"Uh-huh."

"This is Detective Norris. I'm here with Detective Charles."

"Uh-huh."

"Well, sir, we're wondering if you maybe got our last message on your machine. Called ya again about coming down to the station and talking to us?"

"Mmm."

"It sounded like your machine might've got filled up there and cut off the last bit of what we said. So, we wanted to try you at home one more time and nail down a date for…"

"For?"

"Follow-up questions. *—No, I ain't gonna ask…Lee, you want me to say it? Fine.*— Questions about your grandson and the incident."

"Mmm."

"At Camp Arrowhead?"

"…"

"Mr. Grimsby?"

"Boy's shook up by it all. By everything that happened there. All them dead kids around. Good kids too. Probably. And him the sole survivor."

"—*Did you also just hear him say probab*— …And the girl also, Mr. Grimsby. Sir. Alison Vesta survived as well. She's still in that medically-induced coma. But we hear through the grapevine that she's improving. Winter formal's in a few months at the high school. Wouldn't that be a sight, Alison Vesta in a wheelchair or maybe walking with some crutches. Not a dry eye in the gymnasium, I bet. Might be she'll wake up sooner than that and fill in some details for us, help us figure out for certain what happened out there that night."

"That so?"

"There's always hope."

"Boy got cut bad, too. There's a big scar across his belly now. Ugly damn thing."

"—*I'm getting to it, Lee.*— Mr. Grimsby, you still there? Listen, sir, we don't wanna talk to the boy…I mean Clint. Not just yet. We wanna talk to you. You see, we're wondering if maybe you noticed anything or if Clint's said anything to you about what went down at Camp Arrowhead. Or if maybe he's even done anything to give you the impression he remembers something from the incident. Something he failed to mention to us?"

"Mm."

"Mr. Grimsby…you mind if I call you Roger…what time can we set up a meeting for…? Mister…? —*Shh. Shh. Shiiit. Sunuvabitch left the goddamn telephone off the hook. He's making breakfast now…frying bacon…shit.—*"

A long time's passed since Roger smiled. But the sizzle and pop of the thick-cut bacon on the skillet underscored by the mumbled cursing from the phone brings him as close to a grin as he's come in years.

Roger beats a rapid-fire tattoo on the boy's black-painted bedroom door. Clint's dad picked the color when he was filling the role of the sullen, long-haired teen living under the Grimsby roof. Roger still remembers the name on the can of paint. "Perfect Midnight." He recalls asking his son, "What's a perfect midnight supposed to be anyway?"

"God, Dad, shut up."

As good an answer as any for such a dumb fucking question.

But he was a father then and some level of moderate teasing and needling felt like a necessary function of the role.

Clint sticks his head out from the room, disheveled hair like hedgehog spikes and black rings under his eyes to match his grandpa's. "Yeah, Grandpa Roger?"

The old man leans forward on his moccasins. But he holds back from going onto full tip-toes because he's not sure his liquor holds the way it used to and he'd hate to go sprawling in front of his grandson. There's nothing much inside the bedroom except for the detritus of youth. Dirty clothes, yellowing pieces of wadded-up toilet tissue, half-drunk Coca-Cola cans.

Nothing suspicious here.

Clint steps into the hallway, letting the black door shut behind him. "You got a phone call? Another journalist, huh?"

"Nah, damn telemarketer."

"Mmm."

Well, now I know what it sounds like.

"Got the griddle out, set it to heating up on the wood stove. Made some flapjacks and extra-crispy bacon for us."

There's the ghost of a grin on the boy's face. Like his body's re-learning how to enjoy things. *Or like he's faking it.*

"Great. I could sure kill a stack of flapjacks. With extra maple syrup."

The back porch screen door slams shut, and this time Roger *does* hear his grandson's feet on the gravel, the car door opening, and the old Mustang roaring to life.

Glad the boy's going out. Good for him to get out in the world. To see folks and let folks see him. Gotta get in front of what they're no doubt already saying. Can't let 'em make up their own tales about him, about what happened. Wouldn't be right…

Roger glances at the yellow notepad where he keeps his official, though by no means pretty or easy to decipher, painting commission records. One of the art directors, an old-school gal he imagines always takes a scotch with every lunch she eats up in New York City, told him horror books were enjoying an unexpected resurgence among readers and book-buyers alike, hence the increased demand for his work. "Not that I understand it! People are scared enough with the way the world is going these days," she'd said.

But Roger disagreed. "We'd always rather be scared by the shadow on the wall than of the thing making the shadow," he'd replied, impressed by his own answer. Like he knew what the hell he was talking about well enough to hand down such fortune-cookie aphorisms.

He's got a few pieces with approaching deadlines to mail out, so he's heading into town later to drop them at the post office. A lot of presses ask him if he'll work digitally, but Roger tells them it's like asking if he'll ever flap his arms and fly. Sometimes tradition wins out and there's no chance of evolution. *I'll stick to the muck I call home, thank you very much!*

No blue-sky morning for Roger, a storm's moved in by the time he reaches town. A thick, black wall of rain-heavy clouds encases the city proper, making Roger suspect the previous night's dark skies won't relinquish their control. Driving along, he finds a welcome committee of empty streets to greet his arrival. Not even one sad person is visible, no one with their coat pulled over their head as they dash for a nearby parked car.

At an intersection, Roger notices graffiti spray painted in huge black aerosol-blasted shapes across the plywood boards nailed in place over the old art supply store's windows. *THE MOON MAN'S WATCHING*, the dripping letters declare.

The store used to be the place where Roger ordered all his brushes, paints, pencils, erasers, and more. But its loss doesn't cross his mind too much these days. He gets Clint to order new supplies for him on the computers at the town library whenever his materials run low.

The store's been gone for a while, but the words scrawled across the planks appear to be new.

THE MOON MAN'S WATCHING.

Roger checks out of the pick-up's back window. No one's there but his reflection, which is disrupted by the wriggling worms of splattering raindrops, and the slick, shimmering blacktop stretching behind him, its asphalt face scarred by staccato lightning bolts of fading yellow paint. Focused back on the task at hand, he pushes his foot down with practiced deliberateness, so the tires don't spin and send him slaloming on his way.

Driving ahead, he listens to the rain on his windshield and the water splashing from his tires, like he's eavesdropping on the conversation of strangers conducted in a foreign language. When he notices the signs for Mercy General Hospital and not the cracked parking lot of the post office, he's not surprised.

Well, this isn't where I wanted to go, but maybe it's where I'm meant to go.

"She's improving," that one detective said. Talking about the girl they found alive with Clint.

His blood on her and her blood on him.

Damnedest thing.

When the authorities described the scene to him on that breathless morning where every word came like the speakers didn't believe them even as they spoke them, Roger's mind focused on the colors he'd use to paint the scenes as they were laid out for him. Burnt umbers, glimmering royal blue, yellow ochers blending with peach and velvet at the sight of the entry wounds. Dark black streaks framing the teens and a pale white light washed over them from the front. While he sat and listened, Roger's hand moved like it had a mind of its own, crawling across the tabletop until it found the nub of an old pencil and a scrap of paper. This sketch of his bloody grandson and the girl marked the first piece of art he'd made in years that wasn't for a commission.

Nothing more than art for art's sake.

Roger sits with the ignition off in the back of the hospital parking lot, letting rain cascade around his truck. He goes over the details of the initial call as he received it on that humid summer evening when the cricket string quartet played sharp notes among the tall blades of grass. "Something happened at the Camp."

Roger's mind can't help but wander along to the TV crews and the story-hungry reporters swooping into town, plus the politicians, big and small, using the deaths of all those children for justifying their support of one cause or another, then all of them getting bored and pulling up stakes once they grasped how small the town they'd landed in really was and how little impact the deaths—even as lurid and bloody as those from the 'Camp Arrowhead Atrocity'—would have on the wider world, where stabbed and chopped white-bread teens didn't move the ratings needle too much.

Wait around long enough and some no one will get all geared up and shoot as many "some bodies" as he can because no one'll touch his willy and that'll steal the headlines for a week…or a day. Sure seems like it gets shorter and shorter every time.

The boy's wounds healed, leaving the scars on his stomach—showing how *whoever* got him stuck him good but not good enough that he wasn't able to breathe on his own when the paramedics arrived. The injuries appeared rough and ragged-edged to even an untrained eye, but they'd also all landed nowhere near any vital organs.

The coma girl's mother stands under a gazebo set up a short distance from the hospital. The pebbled ashtray cemented nearby overflows with butts. The woman seeks to contribute, balancing a thin Virginia Slim on her trembling bottom lip and rummaging through her clutch. Her hands come back empty and tears cling to the edges of her long, curling lashes, sitting thick as the raindrops fall beyond the structure's curved awning.

Thin white hairs plastered to the top of his head, his denim jacket turned a deeper, darker blue thanks to the downpour, Roger steps forward, out of the rain. His Zippo's out, and his thumb's poised, ready to strike the flint. He's watched the woman long enough through the front windshield of his pick-up to figure out what she needs.

The girl's mother—Roger knows her name's Jeanie on account of all the news reports—forms her mouth into a surprised circle. Her lipstick's a smear against her chin like she got interrupted during its application and her urge to smoke overwhelmed any clean-up attempts.

"Ma'am," Roger says, trying to match his drawling intonation to some charming cowboy helping out a damsel in distress. But a crack of lightning and a boom of thunder overhead swallow his words, lessening whatever impact he'd intended.

Before Roger's hand comes too close, someone strikes it, clubbing away the offered lighter. The metal skids across the cement, like a skipped stone against the still surface of the millpond.

That'll be the father then.

The not-quite-dead girl's daddy places himself between his wife and Roger. Puffed up with enough spite and venom to make the elder Grimsby keep his distance.

"What the hell're you doing here, old man?"

Silent, Roger makes his face a blank, a mask.

"Grandson of yours…he tell you what happened yet? He tell you all about what *he did* out there? Bet you done a lot of talking with him, huh?"

Still, Roger doesn't say a word. He listens. He wonders how much this angry man knows about where he and Clint live. He wonders about the high beams on the man's vehicle. *Are they champagne color, foaming white with electric power or are they pale, haunted like the surface of the moon?*

When it is time to speak, Roger chooses his words with care. "Understand your daughter's doing better. Considering what our families *both* went through, I figured I'd come here and pay my respects."

The father's hand, palm flat against Roger's chest, pushes the old man out from under the gazebo and back into the rain.

"We don't want your respect. We don't want your help. We don't want your pity. Go ask your grandson what happened. Go ask what he did to our daughter and all those other children. Have you done that yet, huh?

"You know my Mama warned me about your family when I was growing up here, told me all about you painting those awful things for those books…devil's work. Satanic! And that Richie…we're all glad he left town again…"

His wife abandons her cigarette, flicking it out into a puddle at Roger's feet. The pale smoke curls up to the cuffs of his pants. The woman grips her husband's arm tight, pulling him away from further confrontation. "Come on, let's go back inside…"

"I need a drink," the weary father says, never taking his eyes off the old man onto whom he's focused all his unchecked frustrations.

Roger doesn't reply to the torrent of abuse directed his way. In silence, he retreats further into the downpour, carrying the father's anger with him.

The detectives look like children to Roger, waiting by the mailbox he hammered deep into the ground across from the turn-off to his driveway long ago. Both men stand near their sedan, city-issued based on its throwback quality, wearing matching green parkas a couple of sizes too large even for their bulky frames. Roger pulls his truck beside them and reaches across the console to the passenger window, cranking the handle to roll it down.

"Mr. Grimsby, Roger. Fancy meeting you here," one of them—Detective Norris or Charles—says.

"Mmm."

Roger sits back against his seat. The truck's hazards blink in the rain. The ticking mechanism inside the cabin goes *click, click, click, click*. Like the *60 Minutes* stopwatch playing on Sunday evenings.

"We thought we'd bring the party, so to speak, to you. Got time for a few questions? Let's drive to the house and we'll find somewhere to chat. Oh, and is your grandson home by any chance?"

The detective talks a lot, squeezing out too many words with each exhalation. *He's smarter than he looks in that case. Knows his time with me is limited.*

Roger shakes his head. Then, to back it up, says, "No."

"No? No, what? No, your grandson's not home? Or, no, we can't talk?"

Roger faces front once again, but tracks the detectives from the corner of his eye. He turns off the hazards. Then, he throws the truck into drive but leaves his foot on the brake.

The other detective, whichever one's not spoken, clears his throat and clamps his hand on the open passenger-side window. "Wanna hear something they left outta the papers? Something we didn't even share with the families of the deceased because we felt it might be…too traumatizing? Sure, most of those kids got stabbed. Over and over like someone had it in for 'em something fierce. But still…for some of those campers, the killer took *his* time. Not stabbing. Well, not *only* stabbing. But carving pieces off them too. According to the coroner, some of those kids…were still alive when *he* cut them. Like a god-damn deli-counter butcher."

Roger lets the truck roll forward. Both detectives roar, like he's run over their toes. Like they'll find some way to shout louder than the wind and rain in order to get the driver's attention. "Get off my property!" Roger shouts back into the maelstrom. Even though he's got as much chance of being heard and understood as the detectives, he still relishes the resulting feeling of exhilaration. He gives the steering wheel a sharp turn and speeds up his driveway, kicking rocks, dirt, and pine needles behind him.

Of course, part of him hates storming off like that, letting his frustration show through so blatantly. It reminds him of a baby, kicking up a tantrum. Screaming so someone will acknowledge his existence.

When he gets to the house, there's a note Scotch-taped to the front door, its presence illustrating how far the two detectives actually came onto his land before they set up stakes by the mailbox, playing like they needed or were waiting for his permission. Roger pulls the folded page free and opens it. Wet thumbs stain the white paper. But the detectives' words show clear even when the water turns the lined sheet translucent. *"How well do you know your grandson?"*

When Richie came home with Clint, he left the care of the young child to his parents. Mostly that meant Alma, Roger's wife. But Roger wasn't immune to having to pick up the parenting slack from his neglectful son. By then, with the horror book market flatlining and commission work drying up for his macabre masterpieces, Roger put serious consideration into making the switch to painting generic landscapes, the kind of earnest pabulum designed to fill spaces on the walls of hotels and restaurants with homey atmospheres. He knew of at least one artist, close to his age, who'd made a real name for himself with those paintings. Before the artist—Varmette was the man's surname—passed away, he'd even parlayed his Hallmark card canvas success into setting up an annual painting camp he ran with his own son down at the seaside every year. Roger had thought about attending, but never for very long.

Quite an impressive racket if you can get into it, Roger always believed. But he stopped short of falling into full-fledged jealousy. After all, he'd never had any true desire to leave the woods he called home. He'd burn up with too much sun exposure, and the millpond was quite enough water for him.

All the time Richie could've spent feeding, changing, or playing with his son, he'd instead given over to playing his guitar, to working on his *compositions*. The hiss of the amp behind the Permanent Midnight-painted door sounded like a nest of snakes stirred into a venom-spitting anger orgy. Sometimes, the Grimsby patriarch swore his son had long abandoned any notion of *trying* to play something resembling a *tune*. Instead, Richie crafted these piercing waves of feedback bouncing from guitar to amp and amp to guitar. When the *music* grew loud—or louder at least—Alma cleared her throat and gestured first to Roger and then to the black door, like she expected her husband to do something about *it*.

"A father needs to spend time with his son," she'd say.

It wasn't lost on Roger that what she said might have multiple applications.

But he let her comments go, ignored the jabs from the woman he loved. And Richie, he stayed locked away in his room with the roar of static becoming something the rest of the family had to learn to live with. Until it turned into so much white noise.

Of course, Roger grasped his son's true intentions. He understood the effect the lost, dispirited young man hoped to achieve through his sonic experimentation. "Artist to artist," he *got* it. From that perspective, something as culturally advanced as *words* couldn't possibly get the job done when it came to encapsulating their son's work and translating it for Alma.

Baby Clint didn't seem to mind his daddy's music that much. He'd coo to himself in time to the strident thrumming of the cords, his gurgles sounding like the cry of a whip-poor-will. Only one person in the house was bothered by the sounds, and Roger hoped his wife would come to understand and learn to live with it.

But as the dishes and dirty laundry piled up in the hallway, shoved out past Perfect Midnight by Richie when no one was around to see him emerge, the furrow in Alma's brow grew ever deeper.

Roger considered himself a simple man, but far from a naïve one. He grasped the distance between his wife and the art his son was making. He also understood the pain his boy must have felt, trying to share his work with someone he loved who would never understand what he'd made or what it meant.

Things reached a head one summer evening, when Roger took the baby for a walk around the property. That night, the moon hung heavy over the trees, like a pregnant woman's third-trimester swollen belly. Except the satellite was drained of life, an alabaster casting of the real thing.

When they finished the circuit and the child's chubby cheek rested on his grandfather's shoulder, drool staining the fabric of Roger's shirt, the house was quiet. Something had finally made Richie stop playing.

Roger climbed the porch steps two at a time, shoved his way inside the house, and beelined for his son's room. Even before he got there, Roger knew what he'd find.

When he opened the bedroom door, baby Clint awoke and made another of his delighted gurgling sounds. Too late to turn the boy away or shield his wide-open eyes, Roger caught him wriggling his chubby fingers at the shadow shapes before them. Like the child wanted nothing more than to hold the darkness closer.

"Look what I made, Dad," Richie said.

When Roger opened his mouth to scream, his voice was lost over the emergence of static. A tidal wave crested over the house and slammed back down over everything. Everything they'd made, built, and created. It washed away the sins of the son *and* the father.

At least, that's what Roger wanted to believe.

The rain lets up after an hour. But Roger's anger over the two cops coming onto his land hasn't subsided in the least. Staring out from under his front porch awning since he got home, Roger rolls his neck, loosening up the best he can. Neck bones pop like heavy boots in a dry forest, stepping on every broken twig along the way. The temperature drop after the downpour is unmistakable.

Roger knows he should go inside and get his old parka from the coat rack. The last thing he wants is to get another lecture from his doctor about the dangers of pneumonia at his age. Like he doesn't know *all* the dangers he faces each and every single day by heart. So, it's *doctor be damned* as far as he's concerned.

He stomps across the yard, heading toward the trees bordering his land. He's worried the detectives might've snuck back on his land, maybe to bug the property or just to ambush Roger and pepper him with more intruding, busy-body questions. Those hypothetical notions alone enrage Roger, so he pays no mind to the splatter of grass and mud at the cuffs of his jeans.

The world's darker when he steps into the woods. Quieter, too. If he never turns around, then he won't find his house standing tall and ever-present. It'll be like he's walking into an enchanted forest from a fairy tale. The kind with dark trees like shadows and the birdsong of crows serving as a warning to all trespassers. Rainwater left behind from the recently dissipated storm pitter-patters off skeletal branches to moisten the dead leaves carpeting the forest floor.

Instead of a crunch, the damp debris crumples on contact with the tread of Roger's boots. Flies buzz past, darting and dipping, like barnstormers putting on an aerial stunt show. Silver wings tickle the white hairs in Roger's ears.

But there's no sign of the detectives.

Kicking himself for letting paranoia get the best of him, the old man follows the flies congregating in minia-ture storm clouds around him. He figures there's some dead animal nearby, something one of the neighbor's coon dogs got a hold of. He pulls in a deep breath through his nostrils, searching for the scent of blood intermingling with the rainwater.

It's hard to pinpoint anything when the buzzing's so loud. In addition to the flies, gnats and whining mosquitoes soon join the party. Roger waves his hands in front of his face, brushing aside the winged assembly.

He steps into a clearing. A near-perfect circle around which trees grow. Inside, there's usually nothing.

This time, however, something's planted in the obsidian soil. Waiting for Roger's discovery.

Wooden figurines arranged in a tighter circle occupy the center of the clearing. Each figure's around the size of a beer can in height but cut down skinny enough to hold in a closed fist without bulking. Each one displays the harsh angular features meant to represent the carver's interpretation of bodies and heads, faces. With no smooth curving lines, these figures make the sharpness of their creation a feature rather than a defect.

What the hell's this then?

Roger continues his running commentary as he drops to a half-crouch near the ring of wooden figurines.

Don't wanna get my ass wet, he says to himself.

Liar! You wanna stay away from the damn things…

As if to prove his inner monologue wrong, Roger stretches until his fingers close around the nearest figurine. One's enough since they're all more or less the same. Whoever carved this icon repeated the same image over and over. Once he's holding his selected figure in both hands, Roger steps away from the circle. His thumbs and fingers move across the strange object in his grasp.

Bark's peeled away from the wood and the carver used a blade to smooth out the naked wood as they made their alterations. From the large forehead to the sunken cheeks to miniature fists like anvils, Roger's surprised when his hands emerge splinter-free from the inspection. Whoever worked on the piece took their time and likely had prior woodcarving experience. These pieces are no one's first attempt.

It's good work. Solid work.

He brings the figurine up for even closer inspection. His bottom lip drops, and he whistles. Despite the primitive appearance, there's distinct craftsmanship on display.

Roger suspects there's no coincidence or mere chance behind his discovery of the icons. *There are never accidents in the art.* With the same level of certainty, he believes further study of the carving will only serve to strengthen the suspicions he has about a link between the coarsely-rendered wooden features and something living, someone he knows. Someone he hasn't seen for quite some time.

He remembers his son's music, the shrieks and discordant melodies suggesting something grandiose if the listener had the patience to wait it out. The sum more than equaling the parts. The woodwork in his hands reminds him of those compositions. Back then, Roger knew the answers would come with time.

He just never *got* that time.

Circumstances might've changed, but Roger reminds himself that the details below the surface will coalesce in the same fashion. *Whoever* made the figurines would realize their potential. It wasn't a question of *if*, but *when*.

But it's not time yet. This art is not ready to share with a larger audience. What I've got here is still a work-in-progress. A well-made draft, but a draft nonetheless.

Roger squints and checks his watch. He's surprised to find so much time's passed since he stepped across the tree line.

Too much time.

He shoves the single figurine into his pocket and returns to the house. It's closing in on suppertime.

Roger stands on one side of the kitchen island, facing the stove and stirring the broth he's heating for their soup. Clint's on the opposite side of the counter, chopping carrots and celery, and shredding the chicken thighs that Roger seared on a pan moments before. The boy's slow and methodical with his knife work.

Blade goes up, blade comes down.

Roger clears his throat. His grandson tilts his head in the old man's direction. But the smooth, steady movements of his knife-bearing hand continue their unceasing work. "Went by the hospital," Roger says, the words heavy on his tongue.

"Mmm."

The old man presses on. "They say the girl. The Vesta girl…Alison…they're saying she's coming out of the coma they had to put her in."

"Huh."

Blade goes up, blade comes down.

"Her daddy's torn up about it. And…believe me…I understand. Lord knows your daddy…he'd sure hate how you ended up after that."

"Like you, Grandpa?"

Roger stirs too hard. Hot water splashes out of the pan and hits his wrist. "Goddammit!"

Then, recovering, he answers. "Yeah, of course. Of course."

Blade goes up, blade comes down.

"Never learned too much about what you were working on there before the, umm, well…before…you know. Guess kids these days ain't writing letters home from camp, huh? And I ain't checking any texts or emails or tweeters, so…yeah. I never got to ask what you did at that camp before you…"

Blade goes up…

"I recall from the catalog in the mail something 'bout woodcarving lessons. Seemed like that might be something up your alley…"

Blade comes down.

"Whittling's a fine way to pass the time. Fine, fine way. If you wanted…"

The boy's fast even with his gangly limbs in a seemingly never-ending growth spurt. He comes around the island, eyes lit up with intense rage. Roger's old man Adam's apple bobs up and down with a comedic slowness.

Comedic, if only his grandson's hand gripping tight on his shoulder didn't follow.

Clint pushes Roger. The stirring spoon falls from the old man's grip and clatters against the stovetop. His back strikes the island countertop at a slight diagonal. As a result, the sharp features of the figurine press into Roger's flesh through the thin fabric of his pocket. Like the white-faced miniature is sinking its teeth into his worn, wrinkled flesh.

"What the hell're you implying, Gramps? Huh?"

Clint's voice comes loud and strident from his lanky frame. But it doesn't break. No cracks echo in the delivery, as he demonstrates the childhood he's leaving behind and previews the man he'll soon become.

Son of Roger's son. His flesh, his blood.

"I got stabbed too, ya know!"

Still holding his grandfather against the island with one hand, Clint uses his other to pull up his t-shirt. The criss-cross scar tissue pattern across his belly is puckered, pink and white. "You ever stop and look at this? You ever wonder who cut me? Or *what?*"

The boy stomps out of the kitchen. "Fixings are ready for the soup. You're welcome!" With those final words shouted behind him, Clint prepares to make his exit from the house.

When he's out of sight, Roger turns and picks up the butcher's knife. He slips it into the knife block.

The front door slams.

Roger turns the knob on the stove's burner to low and leaves the soup to simmer in the pot. It'll keep for as long as it takes to fetch Clint from the front yard, or so he figures.

When he steps outside and down the porch steps, Roger's thrown by the immediacy of the night. Too late, he's soon looking back from the driveway and finding that he's left the lights off in the front of the house. As a result, the building becomes one more blob of darkness on top of more darkness.

First, the cops, then the figurines…how much time passed after that?

A queasiness rises from his stomach and tickles his throat. He swallows it back. A loud rattling cough follows.

The coughing stops, but a squelching, like heavy feet on damp leaves, echoes from the tree line. Roger tries to pinpoint the source. His eyes aren't what they used to be though. It's one of the reasons why he gave up hunting.

Couldn't hit a damn thing. And didn't much enjoy coming home empty-handed.

Plus he never cared for the company of the other men out there in the deer stands and duck blinds. The one time he brought Richie out, when his son was entering the early days of his angsty teenage years, the boy spent the whole time complaining about the cold and the quiet. On and on, until Roger stood up and trudged back to his truck with nothing to show for their time together. Richie followed behind, making these deep, chest-clenching sobs, like his father had screamed at him and whipped him to boot. Roger never tried hunting with Clint. Didn't even consider asking his grandson if he wanted to go.

The face peers from between the pines, impossible to miss. Round and beyond pale, a chalk-dust white rather than any known skin pigment, with eyes of sky-blue shot through with crimson lightning bolts of burst blood vessels. Spying that strange face in the woods, Roger retreats to his house.

When his feet touch the walkway, he's hit by a sudden jolt of adrenaline. The spike building within him since he stepped outside transforms into an invading presence, a sleeper agent activated, breaking the old man's concentration. His eyes are on the front porch and his mind's consumed with questions. *Should I have my gun? Should I get my gun? Wait…*

The sudden silence behind him causes Roger to return his attention to the tree line. The strange-looking face has gone away.

"Goddammit."

Too late for his gun to make any difference, Roger sets out to check behind the house, desperate for answers. Craving confirmation of long-simmering suspicions.

Roger's keyring proves a more useful tool than his gun would have, allowing him to unlock the back door of the house and return to the safety of his dwelling. His boots and pants have come through their nighttime trek soaked by mud. He doesn't stop at the mat to scrape the detritus of the yard from his treads. Instead, he grinds the earth into the carpeted hallway as he marches back to the front of the house.

"Clint? Clint?" He whispers his grandson's name, soft and sweet like the awful years never happened and they're back playing hide-and-seek. All he's doing is giving the boy more time to secret himself away. Offering a final warning: *Ready or not, here I come…*

But there's no Clint. The open front door awaits Roger as he finishes traversing the first floor. He grips the doorframe, one hand on each side. His heart thumps, a caged beast ready to wreak havoc if the bars ever loosen.

Or he's the caged beast, ready to give up the ghost and lay down to die…

Everything hurts in ways it used not to. He wants to turn around, close the door, and retreat to the starch-stiff blankets tucked Army tight to his bed.

But when he grabs the door to pull it shut, Roger comes to understand that it's not so easy to let these things go.

He's never feared the voices.

Except this time, when they ask, *Did you close the front door before heading into the woods? Or did you leave it open like this?*

Huge blue and red fireflies spin between the trees, far from Roger's porch. The police cruisers' swirling lights come one after the other, after the other. Sirens wail, like banshees' cries outside the windows of the dying. Shrill heralds of misfortune. There's no one around to assure Roger the lights and sirens are moving *away* from his house, driving *past* his turn-off. He can't bring himself to believe: *They're not coming here. They're not coming for you.* Doubt threatens to eat him from the inside out.

He doesn't wait for that to happen though. Aging body be damned, he steps off the porch once more, and, this time, runs down the driveway, desperate to catch up to the lights. If he can watch them drive past and see their true destination, then he can rest easier.

When Roger reaches the main road, he's sweat-soaked and shivering, stumbling through the darkness. He curses himself for leaving without a flashlight as he's had to re-learn how far the backwoods void-space spreads under the canopy of pines. Navigating the darkness at his age has proven to be a taxing experience, mentally and physically. Time slips away from him, even faster than it usually seems to. When he steps from gravel and onto smooth, flat asphalt, the old man releases a long, low breath like he's letting his soul escape on the exhale.

A flashlight's beam, like a miracle Roger didn't dare pray for, cuts up the darkness along the roadside. "Mr. Grimsby? Roger? 'zat you?"

When Roger turns to the speaker and the light, he's met with the low, steady growl of a hunting dog. A chain rattles. Then, a snap follows as the lead's pulled tight.

The woman speaks again, but not to Roger.

"Dammit, 12, hush your ass up." A yelp comes next and the dog goes quiet. Its master turns her flashlight up, holding it under her chin like a pre-teen telling campfire ghost stories.

Georgia Brandon's a widow. Her deceased husband was a poacher and drunkard who'd crashed his car on the roadside between their two properties. He'd flown through his front windshield and got cut up bad.

Head one way, body the other.

She kept the house in the woods and her husband's hunting dogs as well.

"You okay, Roger?"

Her dog whimpers and she pulls on the chain, nearly dropping the flashlight. The light jiggles under her wobbly chin. *It's been a rough few years since her husband's accident.*

Roger nods. "Yeah, I'm good. Winded's all. What's happening?"

"Something or other went down up at the old honky-tonk…"

"So, it *is* still open…"

"What?"

"Nothing, go on. You were saying something happened?"

"I was chasing this fool dog and he's 'bout to go high-tailin' further down the road to go splashing around in the millpond when those cruisers came racing by. Thank the Lord I managed to grab him by the dang collar 'fore he got out on the road. I was worried they'd run us over. Funny thing though, with all them lights flashin' I could see straight to the honky-tonk parking and I swear there's one car of theirs already there. Detectives' sedan, you know? Couldn'a been much help for whatever went down there though. I walked closer and watched 'em pulling enough of those black bags out to fill a few pews at church, yeah? Horrible, just horrible. Before I could even get one word out to 'em, one of those little junior deputy-types told me to go home. Can you believe that? No goddamn wonder everyone hates the motherfucking police these days. Incompetent assholes!"

Roger nods. His house becomes a magnet—pulling him toward the quiet security it's provided for years.

"Gotta go…" he mutters.

As Roger plunges back into the abyss, the Widow Brandon calls after him. "Well, bye, then!"

Her throaty chuckle, a cheap amateur-hour Mae West, gets overwhelmed by her barking dog. Both sounds fade into background noise and then dissipate to nothing at all. Darkness smothers sound and narrows vision. For most of the long walk back, Roger focuses on the basics. One foot in front of the other, trying to stay in a straight line while traversing the rough terrain of the driveway. Walking down it once was bad enough, the trip back is pure hell.

Except sometimes, there *is* light. Sometimes, when Roger glances to the right, to the side closest to the trees, the quiet, pale stranger's face returns. It watches him from the forest.

At first, he ignores its presence. Some instinct reinforced by years of living in the middle of nowhere tells him, *If something bad's gonna happen to ya, then it'd already have happened.* He's determined to leave the stranger alone, to let it keep pace with him from between the trees.

When his truck is in sight and his return trek's almost ended, Roger grows bolder, more daring. He steps off the gravel and heads for the trees. He doesn't call for the stranger. He pretends to let them be, and walks with his head up and his eyes clear. Like there's something else in the woods that's grabbed his attention, something other than the strange white peering out from the trees. It's a terrible performance he gives, so Roger's not surprised when his efforts prove fruitless.

When his foot crosses the tree line and his hands reach for where he thinks the stranger's hands should be, there's no one there.

Like a thin film of smoke dispersed by a whisper.

Roger finds the house as he left it. Quiet and dark.

Circling the house, checking for the bone-white stranger hidden somewhere on the grounds, Roger scoffs at the black-out curtains hanging in his grandson's windows. He believes it's dark enough, without needing to help things along.

Inside, Clint's black door exists as an endless abyss against the plain, powder-colored walls.

Standing before it, Roger again imagines the darkness has crept into the house behind him and gained more than a toehold. The old man doesn't knock or call out and wait for a response from within. His hand closes around the cool metal of the doorknob and twists.

He pushes the door open.

Dim light from the hallway shines into the otherwise darkened room.

Clint stands in the doorway. Staring ahead. In stasis. Like Roger's peeled open a cocoon to find a caterpillar catatonic, mid-transformation.

Roger's hand trembles. The spots on his knuckles dance. Then, he slaps the boy's cheek. One swift, decisive strike, before the old man's arm falls to his side.

Already, the splotchy red blob of a handprint is forming on his grandson's face. A mark imprinted, tomato-red against pale skin.

Roger pulls the door closed. He won't check if Clint's okay, won't check if he's weeping like his daddy, or if the young man's even moved at all.

It's enough to pull away with the skin across his hand tight and tingling, pain and confusion burning inside.

Roger will wait until the boy's ready to talk.

He'll wait as long as it takes.

Richie never talked to his old man about their differing creative pursuits. He never let himself get engaged in conversations about the melodies on his electric guitar. Never asked questions about the gruesome, slimy, painted canvases his old man used to create and ship off to the publishers in New York City. Didn't seem to give a good goddamn when those same horrific images Roger painted came back shrunk down and fitted with foil-embossed titles or peekaboo cutaways revealing grinning skulls, sharpened silver knife blades, and bloody-mouthed were-beasts. If his son read any of the books his old man had a hand in creating, Roger never saw any of the evidence.

The sole time Richie ever shared his art with Roger, without obfuscation or embarrassment, was when he'd finished with Alma. The scene inside the bedroom, produced to a score of howling guitar feedback, represented the young man's masterpiece and he'd beamed at his father as he finally had the opportunity to share his *work* with an audience who might appreciate the craft and artistry behind it. Richie left his guitar plugged in, resting against the amp with the speaker volume turned to its max setting. The raging static flooded Roger's ears until he detected the voices beneath those relentless pulses.

No, not voices. One voice. A droning chant pulling everything to it like the tides toward and away from the shoreline.

"What have you done?" he asked.

"I made this for you, Dad. Made it for Clint too. I call it my *Moon Man Sonata*." He reached down and plucked one of his mother's strings. The sound echoed throughout the house, pressing forward into an endless night.

The day's wait isn't so bad.

Roger stays inside, making sure all the doors stay closed. He pushes aside the shades and peers down the long driveway, but no one comes.

Shadows appear around mid-day and grow longer, stronger under his watchful eye.

Roger listens to the radio. Local newsreaders offer breathless updates about the "Honky-Tonk Massacre."

They read victims' names, working overtime to ID bodies after the summer camp incident. They want to give their viewers the impression that they've learned something, that they've grown.

Two detectives. A vengeful father who'd promised—*promised*—his wife he'd stay away from the outskirts of town. Strung-out junkies and winos with nowhere to go except to stumble into death's embrace. Some crackpot calls in the on-air tip line, babbling about how "the Moon Man's returned, after all these years," but they cut him off and apologize for the interruption.

Roger sits at the kitchen table with emptied shoeboxes and pulled-apart photo albums. He's curated a gallery of images on one side of the tabletop. Pictures of his grandson. Smiles, hugs, kisses. Showing off his newest toys with a lopsided grin or pointing to cuts and scrapes with watery eyes and wrinkled lips mid-tremble.

With the last photograph, Roger holds it up for closer inspection. A younger Clint sits at the same kitchen table holding the remnants of a PB&J in his tiny hands. Cherry jam's smeared across one side of the boy's face.

Like Roger's red handprint.

Like blood.

On the other side of the table: every knife or bladed implement that he could find in the house. All butter knives, the butcher's knife, the bread knife, a hacksaw, the set of steak knives saved for special occasions, even pieces of plastic cutlery saved from long-ago trips into town for Chinese take-out. Each blade is laid out side-by-side, like misshapen rows of teeth. Some straight, some curved, some with jagged sides. He's even got out pocket knives and hatchets. A machete used for clearing brush.

Roger's checked, again and again, updating his mental catalog. He's ready to sit back, to breathe. Until he remembers…his X-Acto knife in the studio upstairs.

The chair's creak from his weight shift is drowned out by the click of a black door opening down the hallway.

Clint's door.

The timing's perfect. Lights go out, extending the darkness painted on the boy's door to everywhere and everything inside their home. Roger waits, keeping his hands close.

One breath in, one breath out, then repeat. Until a pale visage disrupts the black.

The face from the woods.

Roger knows this face. He's *worn* this face. He's used this face when necessary. It's the face he created, the face Richie re-created as well, and now Clint's having his turn.

It's a face designed to keep secrets. It's a face that is plain and unspoiled, demanding nothing and asking so little in return for the *use* of its likeness. Like a blank sheet of paper, a melody waiting for its tempo, or a piece of wood, it's nothing more than raw material…a tool used for creating a multimedia masterpiece linked in blood and shared across generations of the Grimsby line.

For us, there simply is no separating the art from the artists.

"Come out here, boy," Roger says, tapping his finger against the tabletop between the old photos and knives—a nexus of possibility.

"Come out," he repeats. "I want to show you how to do this right, so you won't get caught. I tried to show your daddy…but he didn't want to learn. Thought because he made music that his old man, the painter, couldn't help him or offer insights on the art. Your daddy had the talent, but not the discipline. His art was raw, lacking direction. I let him go too long without saying a word. No 'this is good' or 'this is bad' or nothing like it. Looking back now, I *understand* why he did what he did. But I can't condone it. Couldn't then, can't now. He hurt your grandma. Killed her. Probably did the same for your mama, too. Always had a hard time keeping his story straight about what happened to her before y'all came to live with us. I watched him, watching you. You'd squish Play-Doh in between your fingers, but the way you worked it after… You made this face. *You know the one.* If it wasn't for the musky, salty, wheat smell, you'd swear it was real. Your daddy didn't like that. I believe he would've hurt you too."

Roger chokes back a sob, strangling it in his throat before he continues. "Dammit. He just didn't get it. Didn't understand the art's meant for building something, all of us, together. Putting him down was one of the hardest things I've ever done in my life. But it had to happen, so the art could continue…so your contribution to it could develop. I saw it then, but I didn't accept it until what happened at your summer camp."

Creation, destruction…the canvas we're given in life, it's the same in the beginning and at the end. A blank, pale white surface on which hopes, dreams, nightmares, and fears are given shape.

He doesn't share the last part. Some lessons can't be passed along from one artist to the next, from family member to family member. Those insights come from experience alone. They come with getting hands dirty, brainstorming, testing methods and materials until you find the perfect combination, something that brings what's inside your head the closest to reality. In short, it's the creative process in all its bloody detail.

Having said his piece, Roger watches as the pale, silent stranger gathers the knives, taking the tools needed to perfect the art, and then retreats behind the black-painted bedroom door. Rogers knows that he won't be the one to open that door after it closes again. He won't peek inside. As long as he never checks, he won't have to confirm if the stranger's no stranger at all but the boy he loves, the boy who loves him.

But he does bend down and pick up the X-Acto knife from the floor, rubbing a finger across the blade. He moves from silver to crimson stain and back again. Then, he stands back to study the door with the words cut through the wood. Splintered white disrupts the black of a so-called "Permanent Midnight." Words wait for the elder Grimsby.

TEACH ME

The murky darkness inside the house reminds Roger of the impenetrable cold black waters of the millpond. Strange how all those years, all those disappearances from the honky-tonk and the surrounding area, and no one's ever dragged the pond.

It's so long ago now, even the small-town folks obsessing over every detail of their small-town lives don't remember those original honky-tonk disappearances. *Without bodies, without something to show, what's even the point?* They've moved on to the next tragedy, the next sanitized crisis pre-packaged for consumption.

But Roger's always known someone is watching, peering over his shoulders and the shoulders of those who came after, always trying to see what they're creating. Encouraging them to keep going, to never stop—to do more, better.

It's the moon. The lumpen satellite circling the Earth and reflecting light from the sun back onto the planet. The ancient space rock hanging in the night sky and watching. Each phase, a different face, a different flattened expression writ large.

Each one so quiet, so white.

IMAGO EXPULSIO
(THE RED ANIMAL OF OUR BLOOD)
J.A.W. McCarthy

I'm standing in front of the fireplace when the painting begins to vomit.

It starts with a bubble on her lips, wet motion in a mouth about to pop. *Her* because she is a young woman—hair to hips, arms crossed over bare breasts, eyes closed and head slightly tilted back in a moment that might be the advent of slumber or surrender—captured in Baroque admiration on the three by two-and-a-half foot canvas perched above my fireplace.

Finally. This is how she speaks to me, after all these years.

The bubble pops, her lips peeling back and jaw releasing into a gaping yawn. She speaks from that torn-open mouth, long-dried oils crackling and corroding the same way celluloid burns. Black, to yellow, to hot orange. Edges curling, a speckle of holes like pustules, joining and spreading into a cascade that pours over the eight-inch buck knife displayed below it, laps at the mantle, the hearth, my feet too damn close and too damn transfixed to move. If I didn't know better—if I had let time strangle belief—I would blame the paint, something about years of shitty apartments infested with humidity and condensation and mold causing this combustion.

She makes little sound. The canvas never splits, its weave still obscured by layers of an ever-changing mind and assurance and time as underpainting. Thick liquid bubbling, sizzling to the eye only. I get a whiff of wet asphalt, cedar—how it smells when it rains here. The vomit, settled between knick-knacks and mortared bricks and my feet, turns back to black. Dead paint.

I'm both nervous and excited. The waiting became too comfortable, even though I've been ready. Wanting.

It's when I think to grab rags and cleaner that something new slips out of that churning, sparking universe that used to be her mouth. A slim scrap of ghost-white flesh the length of my forearm slides out in a squelch of what could be blood and mucus. Its center is slashed in stigmata. I watch it ride the floor in its afterbirth, stopping only when it hits the bookcase. I shouldn't, but I want to pick it up with my bare hands. I want to feel it.

Because I know what it is. Whose it is. I've touched and tasted and loved that scar before.

Elise and I didn't have any classes together, and no one I knew shared classes with her, but that wasn't unusual; students often drifted in and out of our small art school, and seniors were consumed with finishing up our required Humanities credits and haunting open studio time as we worked towards our final projects. If our heads weren't up our own asses, they were pressed into paper and canvas and wood, woozy from the toxic fumes of our endeavors. We sleepwalked past our classmates in the halls; snippets of skin, blurs of hair, voices smeared in a flurry of deadline-driven motion. We often joked that anyone could slip into a class or take advantage of the facilities, so why were some of us stupid enough to bear the crushing burden of student loan debt? When I first saw Elise, I wondered if she might be one of those clever interlopers, just quiet enough, just unassuming enough to get what she needed and slip out again.

It was not love, or even infatuation at first sight. Her back was to me. It was just before 11:00 p.m. and she was the only one in the paint lab, her and her easel ringed in studio lamps as the shitty fluorescents stuttered overhead.

"Sorry," I said when she jumped at my presence in the doorway. She didn't turn around, but her shoulders jerked, a reflexive straightening I recognized in the back of her neck. "I didn't think anyone would be here this late."

"Can't help when inspiration strikes," she said, punctuating her statement with a little laugh that was either a nervous opening or a polite ending.

I moved to the wall of cubbies and pulled my canvas from the slot where it had been resting untouched for the last week. I had a critique next week, and working during open studio hours wasn't enough anymore. Unlike Elise, I was more comfortable standing on a tarp in my tiny living room than in this crumbling brick building just ten minutes before the paint lab tech would hustle us out.

"I'm just getting my canvas," I said, because she wasn't saying anything. From my position, I could see a sliver of her face, a dash of eyelashes and pursed lips in profile, the lights lifting the auburn and blue tones in her long, dark hair. I didn't know how she could work like that, how she could have all that hair loose without constantly pushing it out of her face and leaving smears of oil paint along her brow and cheeks. Her oversized cardigan and white t-shirt—the cover of the "Man-Size" single with PJ Harvey's slick black bun and the rose in her teeth—and jeans appeared unmarred as well, what I could see from that angle, anyway. Even her canvas was tidy, background brushstrokes ending at the crisp lines of her portrait sketch. I found her neatness validating. I was the opposite of the frenzied artist other students aspired to, all amphetamines and outbursts, paint splattering the walls same as their untamable and unknowable muses. Destruction had never been a part of my process, and for that I'd been called uptight a time or two in critiques.

Canvas in hand, I should've left then, but there was something about this woman who looked so much worldlier than the rest of my classmates. Was she here working this late because she had a family at home? Roommates who couldn't bear the stench of turpentine and varnish? Was she not spending her night at one of the dives ringing the campus because she breathed art instead of bourbon?

I took a few steps back towards the door, the bottom corner of my canvas skipping atop years of dribbled paint crusting the floor. The shiny domes, though scuffed and faded with dirt, still looked tacky, like they'd squish and pop under my shoes. "The lab's gonna close soon," I said. "They're pretty strict about it—the paint tech doesn't give a shit if you'll only be another minute."

At that, she reached into the front pocket of her jeans and produced a ring with two keys. They clinked against each other as she turned around to face me. "Good thing I'm fucking him, then." A toothy grin bloomed across her face as she surveyed my struggling face. "No, I worked out a deal with him. I'm writing his Modern Lit paper in exchange for a week of twenty-four-hour studio access."

"Oh, smart. 'Cuz, yeah, I don't know anybody who would fuck him for this."

She laughed. "Well, if he didn't think he was too good to do the reading, I might've. I can't work at home."

"Roommates?"

It was fleeting—and I could've imagined it—but she flinched. Her features constricted as if she'd been pinched by an unseen hand, then they unraveled again, a gentle flow from her dark messy brows to the harsh line of her nose to her wide mouth and pointed chin.

"I prefer to be here at night," she said.

Nodding, I propped my canvas against the wall and crossed back to where she stood. Now that I was directly in front of her easel, I could see that the white was not a primed canvas but an uneven layer of gesso with her pencil sketch atop. Beneath those layers, I could see faint blurs of pink and brown and red, a face wiped away. Ghost or foundation, I wasn't sure.

"Are you painting over an old painting?" I asked. Many students did that; canvas and stretcher bars weren't cheap and living quarters were too cramped for art school accumulation.

"Not really," she said. "I like a lot of layers."

Layers. Another thing I'd been told my work was missing. Every year, on the first day of classes, our professors had us look around the room, informing us that, ten years from now, only one of us would still be an artist. By the end of my freshman year, I already knew that person wouldn't be me.

I wanted to believe that Elise felt that way too, that despite her obvious talent, she knew she was no different than me.

"I'm Elise," she said, extending a slender hand.

Her grip was firm and warm, the creases in her palm pronounced and rough against my own un-calloused skin. That hand had probably held a paintbrush since she was two, encouraged by free-spirited artist parents who gave her her first taste of red wine and late-night art theory, then released her like a tiger, all bared-teeth and untamed skill, into the world.

I didn't want to let go of that hand.

"Shauna," I said, jolted back into the moment by her grip releasing mine.

"You should join me, Shauna," she said, gesturing at the empty easel to her right. Her sleeve rode up with the movement, revealing a pale pink line that split her forearm from elbow to wrist. "Tell me what you're working on."

I did as she suggested and set up next to her. In that moment, it didn't matter that I'd be here until 2:00 a.m. or later by the time I cleaned up, or that I had an 8:00 a.m. print class. Me with my newspaper clippings and thrift store photographs—my latest attempt at texture and layers and giving in to an accumulation I would later regret—and Elise with a portrait so laborious I could imagine it being stripped and studied in every dissected layer decades from now. I pretended to fuss over mixing paints, but I already knew I wouldn't be able to concentrate. The building was dead, only the creaking of the sagging floor beneath our feet and our own inhales and exhales to mark our presence. Without my headphones—how I liked to work—I was distracted by every small sound, even the scratch of Elise's chin against her shoulder as she seemed to satisfy an itch. Beneath the oils and turpentine, I caught a whiff of cedar and something else, like rain-wet asphalt mixed with spilled gin. It was the city, where we stood now in the perfect pocket between the water and the mountains. Mold too, but that could've been the hundred-and-ten-year-old building. When I yawned, a tang like blood caressed my tongue.

Elise was so focused I wondered why she'd invited me, why I'd accepted instead of dropping off my canvas at home and heading to the bar as I'd planned. I moved my brush around the canvas, listlessly smearing colors in places I hadn't planned. I caught myself staring often. Every time Elise's arm swung with an abrupt dip into her palette, I watched that long straight scar surface and I pictured a shard of metal car door lodged in her skin, or a knife in the fist of a violent ex. She wore it with pride—or indifference. I wasn't sure. I wanted to know what cut her open. I wanted to know if she'd been cut open before.

She was right. All those moments of doubt triggered by impatience and hopelessness and lies told to new part-ners—all obliterated now, smashed into dusty memory by this proof, this scrap of forearm in my hands. I've waited for this moment for twenty years.

The woman in the painting—the one I know but don't recognize—has returned to satisfied repose. She's done for today, but this is enough. Over the years, I would catch a glimpse of her while walking down the hall or from another room, and I swear there were times her eye twitched in a conspiratorial wink. There were times I swear I saw her lips part and I thought this was it, it was finally happening. Drunk or sober, sleep-deprived or well-rested—no matter my state of being, my desire ran so deep I could hallucinate the coming of that long ago promise. I longed—lived—for that acknowledgment, and now I have her body.

It's supple and almost vibrates in my hands. Not dried, not preserved, not leather. Alive. A pale length of skin draped across my palms. Back then, we'd hold our arms out against each other in comparison. She was blue-veined and sun-vulnerable, and I was watery gold striving for sun-brown next to her, a Thai girl fading under Pacific North-west rain clouds. We admired our differences and found comfort in knowing we were the same underneath. We felt the same beneath that thin veneer of skin—I know that now. The underside of this vomited scrap of flesh is slick with a viscous fluid that is close to mucous but slips silky on my fingertips like lube. The smell of the city—sea air, cedar, asphalt—hits my nose as I raise the flesh to my mouth. My tongue finds the scar and traces the ridge that had run from her elbow to wrist, a thin copse of peach fuzz tickling my upper lip. Dulled salt, the bitterness of hand lotion, a quick sweet prick of recognition on the center of my tongue. The smell is the same, but the taste doesn't entirely match my memories. I excuse this difference as a blip, a romanticized skewing of perception. Her skin radiates heat and I sip and slurp until my tongue goes numb. The painting hints at a smile.

Outside, stark white-grey slashes through late afternoon sunlight, threatening rain. The odors of blood and bile rise as the fluids congeal on my mantle and floor, but I'll clean later. Right now, I have to dig.

For the final four nights of Elise's unfettered paint lab access, I joined her. Despite my early morning classes and the unease of walking home alone at such a late hour, I returned to campus each of those nights, lingering in the halls, watching stragglers race the night custodian with their books and tackle boxes in tow. I waited for Elise to enter as the last students left—usually around 10:30—then slipped in five minutes later, pretending it was a delightful coincidence even though we both knew better.

While I forced embroidery floss through the layers of paint and newspaper and old photos I'd affixed to my canvas, Elise patiently worried her own layers. A variation of her face would surface atop the one below, perfectly rendered to my eye, but my subsequent compliment was eradicated by her assurances that it was just another layer— an underpainting and nothing more. Sometimes the woman's face would have Elise's thick brows but a smaller nose, or her nose but a thinner mouth, so I thought perhaps that given night's self-portrait wasn't quite right and she needed to start over. Since I didn't see her using a photograph or mirror as a reference, I wondered if she was trying to create an idealized version of herself. Every night she completed a new woman from crown to lap, then would slap broad strokes of gesso over it, smearing the oils before they even had a chance to form a skin.

"Like pus from an open wound," she said once, eyes sparking with glee.

We didn't talk much on these nights, as if we each feared anything beyond simple acknowledgement might drive the other away, but I liked being near her, as if her dedication and work ethic would rub off on me and carry me to graduation.

During the day, I would wander between classes, slipping into the paint lab any chance I got to check the cubby where I'd seen her place her canvas the night before, its presence proof that I hadn't somehow hallucinated her. I studied the faces in my classes, the halls, the library, to the point of distraction. I lingered on the smoke porch, the parking lot, the admin building, putting off the homework and dishes that were waiting for me in my apartment. I joined a study group that gathered in the various coffee shops and bars surrounding campus solely because I was hoping to see Elise, and when I didn't see her, I found an excuse to leave before 10:30 p.m.

"How many layers are you gonna do? Or is the act the art?" I finally asked her on our last night in the paint lab.

Elise stepped back from her easel and squinted at the canvas, then me, then at the canvas again. My question was meant as a little ribbing—a test of our budding friendship, though I could play it off as serious depending upon how she answered—but the harsh set of her features made me fear that I'd overstepped.

"If we do not consider our every act art, can we even call ourselves artists?" she finally said, raising a hand to her chin. This time, as her loose sleeve slipped down, I was close enough to see the texture of the scar on her forearm, how thick it was, like a sloppy line of beading fusing two lengths of metal together. Her eyes caught my stare and I immediately felt ashamed.

"Shit, no." She laughed, moving her hand from her chin to my shoulder. Her fingers slowly trailed down my bicep before falling back to her side. "Look at your face! I'm not a pretentious fuck, I swear. I'm just here because I can't go home."

Though my face was hot, I laughed with relief. I found an equal amount of comfort and thrill in her teasing. "It's almost three," I said. "Minnie's Diner is open till four."

Slowly, methodically, she rolled her sleeve up to just above her elbow, the full length of her scar catching a sticky shine from the fluorescents overhead. When she did the same with her other sleeve, she revealed a scar on that forearm—this one an angled slash from the mid-arm to elbow—just as thick and sloppy, a savage mark that she seemed to savor revealing.

I was surprised; most people hid their scars, laughed nervously when they noticed someone staring, as if it was a personal failure or a lingering nightmare they didn't want to explain. Because Elise seemed so accomplished and worked so neatly, I couldn't imagine her being accident-prone or clumsy with kitchen knives. Was she simply nonchalant, or were these marks a point of pride? As I continued to stare, she met my rapt rudeness with a smile and swept her long hair into a rope that she tossed over one shoulder. The scar running from behind her left ear to her collarbone was as sculptural and uneven as the ones on her arms. I wanted to touch it. Taste it.

I didn't know if it was her or the ring of lights that were suddenly vibrating a halo of heat.

"Nah," she said. "I'm sick of Minnie's. I'd rather go to your place."

Even after the rain, the earth yields only its top layer. I dig up saturated clumps studded with rocks and tiny roots of weeds before tossing my shovel aside at two feet deep.

It's not a grave, but a mold of a person—space carved for arms and legs spread like da Vinci's Vitruvian Man, a head with extra room for all that dark hair. I've created an inverse approximation of her in my backyard, Elise as a dirt angel.

Flesh will wither to leather in a dry environment, so I coat the shape with a thin layer of potting soil. It feels good in my hands—cool, moist, clumping like biscuit dough in the pinch of my impatient fingers. Twenty years of waiting and damming any doubt and now I'm rough, grabbing, slapping the earth with a frantic prayer that I get what I was promised. I place the sheath of her forearm in its proper place in the Elise-shaped hole and try to fill in the rest with my memories.

Long dark hair, wide mouth, those caterpillar brows that framed not only a bold face but a bold tongue. Her long body roped with lean muscle. I used to admire that length of flesh now in the dirt, how her forearm used to flex with every turn of her wrist as she fucked me. I'd get turned on by the pop of the bright blue vein in her wrist when she wrapped her fingers around a paint brush or even a knife handle. Will all that have atrophied after twenty years inside a painting? Will she emerge from the dirt as she was, or as a middle-aged woman same as me?

With the grey studding my hair and the lines on my face, I'm afraid Elise won't recognize me. How alarming to abruptly wake in a strange backyard, take your first breath in decades, and see a face you can't quite place looming over you. Would she recognize my voice and feel relief at the sound of her own name?

Twenty years trapped in an oil painting. It's a punchline or a classic horror story, maybe a little of both. I don't know if in all that time she could see or hear me. That didn't stop me from talking to her every day, though—some days it was the only time I heard my own voice. The not knowing didn't stop me from showing off a new dress or bra that made me feel sexy, hoping to see a flicker of approval in her painted eyes. It didn't stop me from shying away from a kiss when I brought a woman home, or from taking that woman to my bedroom where I could get what I needed behind a closed door. It didn't stop me from apologizing for those weeks I wore her favorite PJ Harvey t-shirt five days in a row, tears running down my face as I realized all I smelled on it anymore was my own lotion and body odor instead of juniper and city-edged cedar.

I don't care if she was frozen in time or if she's aged like me. All the things she missed—all she knows is me, so I can make this world anything I want for her. We can grow old together, or she can unpause those years and live them now, as long as I'm by her side. I just need her back. I just need to know that after all she's silently witnessed, she still wants me.

The painting watched us.

It remained propped against my front door where Elise had set it, and those dozens of layers of eyes upon eyes watched us because we didn't make it past the couch. She kissed me first, perhaps to shut me up as I nervously apologized for the takeout cartons and half-folded laundry scattered across the coffee table. I kissed her back because it was a relief, a breath released.

Our legs tangled as we hit the couch, then our arms as we fought our own and each other's shirts. I'd never moved this fast with anyone before, never let someone so brazenly invite themselves back to my place, never raced to get my clothes off before the worries about that nights' dinner on my breath or the jiggle of my thighs set in. I hadn't even allowed myself to entertain these thoughts about her those four nights we'd painted side by side. I wouldn't press lest I scare her away, so I let her lead despite my questions. Why couldn't she go home? Was I the only one who knew about her late nights in the paint lab? Did she even go to our school? Perhaps she sensed this and found sex to be the easiest way to distract a curious mind.

Her painting stared at me the way I had stared at her scars. Fascination, helplessness, desire—I couldn't read the stoic expression of the current layer of paint, its brown eyes rolled up in a possible moment of ecstasy that didn't match the tight line of the mouth, the firm set of the jaw. Brushstrokes textured into long dark hair tossed over one shoulder, winding down her side, cupping a bare breast before it pooled atop bare thighs. Same as Elise's hair sweeping over my skin, slipping in and out of my mouth. I could feel that canvas' gaze burning through my naked skin and I couldn't stop sneaking peeks at it. At one point the painted lips parted with Elise's kiss, or so I thought. Muted colors glistened in the low lamplight. Hands emerged and receded. A topographic map of oils and gesso on oils reached towards us, its profile a cake sliced open to reveal its own pressed-thin fat and rubbed-raw paint skin. It unpeeled and fucked as Elise and I did. As my tongue sought every ridge and fold of Elise's skin, the painting hummed with us, vibrating low and insistent against my front door.

Elise never hesitated with my body, but I stopped just short of those beautiful scars. Long, uneven ridges tracing her thighs, her shins, a jagged slash on one buttock, a short thick dash atop one foot. Some were lighter, faded with age, while others were still dark and healing. I moved with restraint, only discovering the tiny marks that marred her hands as I pulled each of her fingers into my mouth. With nothing but the sounds of our breath and the shift of skin on skin, I couldn't risk something as jarring as my teeth catching on her strange seams. I couldn't risk what she might think of me should I savor what I really wanted.

We were fast and furtive as if the painting might tell on us.

"Should I leave?" she asked, after, as I dug a clean t-shirt from the laundry pile and pulled it on. She sat with her legs tucked under herself and her hands on her knees while I hurriedly covered myself, already mired in the knee-jerk shame of my flat ass and soft stomach.

"No, you don't have to." I eyed her red and black flannel at my feet. It was as worn and soft as peach fuzz, and that bloom of humid air and juniper as I had pulled it off her—I longed to go back a couple of minutes, slip that shirt on instead while pretending that it was a convenience or accident so I could feel like a part of her, smell like her, be in her skin. "Stay as long as you like," I offered. "We can get breakfast in a couple of hours."

She smiled. "I know I was forward, but I've learned that you have to be. You have to tell people what you want."

I leaned back into the couch and allowed my hand to brush against her thigh. It wasn't much—a graze of the fat of my palm along a rare patch of unmarked skin—but she quickly placed her hand over mine, guiding it to the dark pink ridge that snaked from her hip to knee. It pulsed at my touch and I thought to pull my hand away, but the urge to feel it was stronger. I struggled to meet her eyes. She nodded.

"Tell me what you want," she said.

When she lifted her hand from mine, I was tentative at first, tracing the scar with a light touch. My fingers fell to either side of it, exploring tiny knots, valleys of smooth ribbon sliding into jagged edges. There was heat and movement under there, probably just blood rushing through veins but what I wanted to be a response to me. I'd never seen or felt scars like these before: brutal and uncontrolled, yet as lyrical and brazen as an Egon Schiele painting.

As I moved to the scars on her shin and calf, they seemed to keen under my hand, and I imagined primordial creatures traversing just under her flesh, seeking sunlight and air. Perhaps no one had cut her open. Perhaps her body was full of things trying to escape, a shiny new version of Elise breaking the surface of worn flesh.

I unfolded her leg onto my lap and kissed the start of a scar at her ankle. I was emboldened by the deep sigh she released as I ran my tongue up to her knee, gooseflesh gently giving way to velvety down like worn flocking on a deer figurine. She seemed to relax even as my lips caught on the little bumps and rough patches of her scar.

My heart pounded in my ears. I knew I should express sympathy for what must have been a life-altering trauma, but I was too greedy to stop this indulgence. The heat in my thighs came flooding back. Her invitation to touch and taste felt as self-serving as my fascination and desire.

"I'm not ashamed of these scars and I wish people wouldn't view them like some tragic secret," she said once I had tasted them all. "I earned them. I want to be admired for that."

"Can I ask who…what happened to you?"

Elise smiled at my hesitation. "There's a man who's been stalking me my whole life. Since I was a kid. Always at night, when everyone's sleeping. Every time, he would attack me."

She paused, and I struggled to organize my budding questions into something coherent and sensitive, to give her the space to reveal what she wanted instead of forcing her to navigate my avalanche of *who* and *how* and *why*. Like those first nights in the paint lab, I was still worried I might scare her away, so I was relieved when she allowed my silence to lay there, then continued.

"I don't know why. I can't be sure, but I think now, I think he wants to crawl inside me, you know? He wants to take me over. It's always the same, though. He shows up and hurts me and leaves. Back then, sometimes he didn't come back for years." She spoke quickly, leaving me still picturing this strange man splitting open her seams so he could crawl inside. "At first, when I was little, my parents believed me. They took me to the hospital. They called the police. But the police never found anyone. They didn't figure how he could have gotten into our house. He kept coming—sometimes he uses a knife, sometimes it's his fingernails. My parents, the police—they started saying I needed help, like I was doing it to myself. So, after a while, I stopped telling anyone. I learned to cover up my wounds."

Some horrible man. Slicing her. His filthy fingers digging in, creating all the clefts I'd kissed just moments before. "I'm so sorry."

She shook her head and pulled my hand into hers atop her bare thigh. "I fought hard. I got good at it. Every one of these—" She guided my hand along the scar on her thigh, then up to a crescent-shaped slash just below her collar bone. Those scars seemed to nudge me, and I realized that I believed her fully, that what I was feeling made it real. "I keep a knife under my pillow. Every scar he's given me, I've done the same to him, just as bad."

"Did you ever…did you try—"

"Stop," she told me, though not unkindly. "He gets in no matter what. I've moved so many times—he always finds me. It's always the same. I can't stop him, but I can fight back."

I glanced around my living room. From the couch, I could see into the kitchen as well as my open bedroom. The kitchen window cut a long shaft of gold from the streetlight across the small expanse, the contents of my crowded cupboards being the only things out of view. There were parts of my bedroom draped in shadow, but I was sure I'd sense movement before Elise's stalker revealed himself. Despite our rush, I'd locked the sole point of entry, the front door. The only blind spot was my bathroom around the corner.

Elise retrieved her shirt from the floor and pulled it on. "Don't worry. He only comes after me at night, when I'm alone."

"It's not that. I—"

"It's okay, Shauna. I'd be scared too, if you don't think I'm crazy." She laughed, a rueful little snort. "I don't care if you think I'm crazy. It doesn't make sense, so I have to be crazy, right? That doesn't change anything."

"So that's why you can't work at home. That's why you're at the paint lab all night."

"Well, I'm out of bribes, so I can't go there anymore. Cafes only work for a couple hours if all you're doing is nursing a cup of coffee. Sometimes I walk, but it's not much safer."

It stung, the thought that she had only come home with me to escape a monster, but I could let that go. I liked her here on my couch, comfortable enough to put her feet up, to bare her body even after the unwinding of pleasure had worn off.

"When was the last time he attacked you?" I asked.

Elise twisted to the side and pulled her shirt down, revealing a three-inch slice parallel to her shoulder blade. The wound had started to knit together, but it was still bright red and sticky, the dotted line of fresh scabs split from our movements. I had kissed her shoulders, gripped the back of her neck… How had I not noticed that? I imagined the weeping fluid on my tongue, the tang and salt of a body intent on healing itself.

"Shit. I'm sorry," I said, rising from the couch. "Let me get you some Band-Aids."

She grabbed my hand and pulled me back down next to her. "I'm okay. I'll be okay. This painting—"

I followed her gaze to the canvas leaned up against my door. Its eyes were still rolled up in indiscernible pleasure or pain, muted skin glistening as if the paint were still wet, hair outlining vague shapes in the shadows. Except now the terse line of its lips was gaping, mouth slack and tongue poised as if waiting to receive sacrament. The woman in the painting who may or may not have been Elise seemed to be holding in a breath, waiting for her next words.

"I figured it out," Elise continued. "I know how to hide."

Now that her forearm is in the earth, the next pieces of Elise come faster.

The painting doesn't stop vomiting. Each time, the woman's lips grip a fat bubble that pops wet with anticipation like a blown kiss. Eyes closed, the paint cracks as her mouth jerks open, a black void giving way once again to hot orange, fluids hissing and spreading, pustules popping in the creeping lava that threatens the mantle, the hearth, the floor. It turns back to black as each new piece of Elise slides out: the flesh from her thigh, her shins, a buttock, a patch of her neck marked with a serpentine scar. All slashed with the dark pink of cells rejoined. Each one awakens a memory on my tongue. I've learned to stand under the painting with my hands cupped, ready to catch each piece as it splatters my face with the wet, sloppy proof of life.

I get them in the ground just as quick. Every ridge gets a kiss, the indulgence of my tongue seeking out the jagged dashes, the satisfaction of a knot interrupting a satiny ribbon of scar tissue still warm and soft and keening at my touch, undoubtedly alive. There's a bitterness, though, same as I found in that first scrap of forearm. It's not unfamiliar, despite my not being able to place it. My tongue loves the sensation of these textures, but not this dulled salt that leeches it dry, makes it go numb as if it's encountered poison. I stick to her with every lick. It's not the tang of blood or the sharpness of pus or any other bodily fluid. It pains me to think that I've forgotten what Elise tasted like, that my memories might be so romanticized I rewrote them into some vanilla sugar fantasy that wasn't even possible.

Yet, she's been inside a painting for twenty years. She's *been* a painting. This strange bitterness must be what stagnation tastes like.

I place each part of Elise's body in its proper place and snuggle them into the cool moist soil. Nothing from her face or torso yet, but it's enough for me to sit back on my heels and admire my work. Back in school I was criticized for my tidiness, my self-control, my unwillingness to destroy. I may have given up painting, but I'm still creating.

Though I'm eager to see her face, I'm not sure I want my memories greeted with a flat mask of distorted flesh, a mess of ragged dark hair trimming hollow skin. I need to see her warm brown eyes open as the pieces knit together. I need to see her teeth in an open-mouthed smile when she recognizes the person who kept her promise, who made her whole again.

It was easy to be with Elise, to make her my focus as classes and critiques faded into a memory from another lifetime. We made our world small and filled with purpose: painting, sex, and protection from the man whose own purpose was endless, senseless assault.

As cocooned as we were, I still waited a week before asking her to describe him, as if doing so might break the spell of our infatuation and send her running. To my surprise, recalling his image didn't seem to bother her. Tall and almost skeletal, with stringy greying hair and pale-blue, almost colorless eyes. A wide, thin-lipped mouth that always hung open in bald hunger. Teeth the same dingy hue as his shirt. Always in a dark fitted suit dotted with moth holes and joints worn to a shine. His face had changed slowly but steadily over the years, Elise explained, as if he had grown with her, aging at the same speed. I pictured Angus Scrimm as the Tall Man as she spoke, though I couldn't imagine him as a young man looming over a seven-year-old in her childhood bedroom.

Though she assured me he would not come to my apartment, would not dare to touch her if we were together, I often found myself peering into dark corners and checking closets. When I suggested we spend the night at her place, she changed the subject.

I thought of sneaking into her building on the mornings she would head home—the only time he couldn't touch her when she was alone, in the daylight—and hiding so I could see how he bypassed locked doors and windows. I fantasized about catching him looming over her sleeping form, knife in hand, how I would be ready with my own knife or a rope slung around his reedy neck. I could almost feel him struggling against my limbs. I could smell sour milk and piss as he went slack in my grip.

Despite her reticence, I believed Elise, but I still preferred the little world we'd made away from school and gossip and endless questions. I had acquaintances but no real friends here, so I wasn't missed at bars and house parties. If anyone had noticed my absence in class, I didn't hear about it. Elise had stopped going to the paint lab at night, so there was no chance anyone I knew would see us together on campus. It didn't matter, though—Elise wasn't my girlfriend because we hadn't discussed if we were indeed together. We simply *were*, and that impermanence and fragility made every moment with her feel as epic as it was indefinable.

Despite the lack of definition in our relationship, I felt protective when I caught people looking at us in coffee shops and diners. I didn't want the fascination and well-meaning concern of others when Elise's scars slipped into view. I didn't want people staring at her, leaning across their tables, eyes flashing and lips parting at the thought of those thick, beaded ridges sliding over their tongues.

I'd never lusted after scars before. When I saw them on past partners, they were merely marks from an innocuous story involving falls off bikes or childhood roughhousing—as forgettable as their origin. Even the cat scratch scar on my last girlfriend's cheek had become invisible to me until we encountered someone's pet cat. I'd never looked at those dark or pale lines and felt the desire to touch them, taste them, feel against my lips the phantom that had cleaved my partner. I had never stayed awake parsing the flavor, feeling my salt-numbed tongue fill my mouth, thinking I could still taste the mineral tang of pus and plasma in the grooves of my molars.

Because of this, I didn't want to fetishize Elise's scars. In the clarity of her absence, I asked myself what I liked about her. She enjoyed music and books and movies just the same as she enjoyed food: in the moment and without shame. I liked how she viewed art with immediate visceral pleasure or revulsion, not hesitating so that she could parse what it meant or why we should or shouldn't like it, like many of my classmates did. I liked to imagine her in a critique, her brief and honest assessments discombobulating the students prone to long-winded opinions meant to show off how much more they knew about art history and politics than the rest of us. Elise had no time for bullshit. She had nothing to prove.

Her scars were as open and bold as she was. Was that it? Admiration? My fantasies fluctuated between me saving her from the man and watching her fighting him off. When we fucked, I watched the lean muscles in her arms flex, the smooth rotation of her wrists and fingers, movements so seamless it was easy to picture a knife in her grip, a blade coming down between ribs or into his taut throat over and over again, the infliction of wounds much more savage than that monstrous man had ever given her. It not only left me in awe but turned me on: her strength, her fearlessness, her confidence and bravery in the face of this unbelievable monster that plagued her, how she fought him for years when others would've given up. I imagined his body was a record of their history, same as hers, but his wounds wept bitter bile and never closed, just crusted over while hers formed beautiful pink ribbons that were satin in my mouth.

She healed herself with his destruction.

So, late one night in my living room, when she finally told me how she would hide from this monster—how she would free herself—I didn't question her, not even when she took the knife to her own flesh.

When I first took the painting, I worried the man who had been hunting Elise would now come for me. He'd been pursuing and assaulting her for years, so why would he stop?

Though the finished painting no longer looked like her, there were versions of her underneath. It was filled with her blood and her body, and it smelled like her, even tasted like her the few times I allowed my tongue to touch a corner of that canvas. I could have never seen that painting before and still known it was Elise in there. The man had known Elise her whole life—wouldn't he recognize her texture, her scent, even better than I did?

Every time I saw a man on the street with the same stringy grey hair and wide thin mouth full of dingy teeth she'd described—even if he wasn't wearing a moth-hole-riddled suit, even if he wasn't tall, even if he wasn't old—I was afraid to make eye contact. Would he see Elise all over my face, or get close enough to smell whatever remained of her on me? Instead, I'd focus on the stranger's exposed skin, searching for a dark line snaking down the length of his neck, a crescent-shaped slash below his collarbone, tiny marks dotting his hands. Elise had assured me she'd given him a matching scar for every one he'd given her. He would be obvious, wouldn't he, even if he was standing on the street instead of in my living room?

The first few years, I was vigilant. I kept Elise's hunting knife under my pillow while I slept, on the edge of the sink while I showered, in my bag when I went out—it was never more than a few feet away from my grip. I checked under the bed and inside every closet after a day out. My diligence may have waned over the years, but I've always had a picture of the man in my mind and I've kept the hunting knife readily available in a place of honor on my fireplace mantle. I still search my home upon every strange sound or shadow, and I'm still disappointed when all I find are my coats in the hall closet and shoe boxes under my bed.

Every blade craves flesh. I stand in front of the painting and think about all the times people asked me if it was mine, if I'd made it. *Who is she?* they asked. I lied every time. There's so much exposed, unmarred flesh on display. An upturned jaw, long neck, arms over breasts, a slice of belly, all that hair—in certain lights they would shift the way her mouth and eyes seem to now, before and after she vomits. I know it's Elise in layers upon layers of disguise, but what if I didn't? What if I could stand in front of this painting with no knowledge of its provenance and allow my naked eyes to search for some shred of familiarity? I place my memories of her mouth, her eyes, her smile over what the paint shows me. I smell the accumulation of the city she used to walk because it's what I know.

But sometimes—at the worst times—I see her lips thin. An exposed tooth is dull, doesn't glint with a painted spark of light like I remember. The color of her eyes has faded, worn away by time or improper treatment of the canvas, I'm not sure. Grey threaded through all that long, dark hair, same as I've been aging. It's on these terrible days that I grab the hunting knife and press the blade's tip against her face. I never break that painted skin, but I push a little. I push until her eyes go dark again and her mouth fills out and those teeth recede. When she sighs, I join her in repose.

Fingers carefully pinching the blade, Elise pulled the eight-inch buck knife from its leather sheath and handed it to me. Stainless steel clip point blade, phenolic handle, aluminum guard. It was surprisingly light in my hand.

"It's the first thing I remember buying with my own money," she told me. "I was eleven? Twelve? Took all my birthday and Christmas money that year. The guy at the sporting goods store thought I was *so* cute, but the whole time I was imagining that blade going through his neck and coming out the other side."

My fingers settled into the handle's three curved indents worn shiny from years of her grip. It was warm, and I felt like I'd been entrusted with something special and intimate, an extension of her body, as if it was fused to her palm instead of in her bag or under her pillow.

"He's always had the same nasty, rusty little knife," she said. "Like a kitchen knife, I don't know. It still does a lot of damage, obviously, but my knife is better. It was made for shit like this. I take care of it, and it takes care of me."

"Have you ever almost killed him?"

Her laugh was rueful, a dark edge to her voice that held me close. "He should be dead. I should be dead. I don't know how any of this is possible. I can't believe you just…believe me."

I felt foolish for a moment, as if I was standing at the precipice of a punchline about to be revealed. *Of course I believe you*, I wanted to shout, though I wasn't sure if that was simply a reflex to keep her here, to keep her wanting me. A monster who only appeared to her, who hurt her for no known reason—of course I had questions, but any doubts I had could be easily pushed aside by her lips brushing the back of my neck, her fingers tracing my collarbone, or, in less intimate moments, the resignation that settled into the hollows of her face whenever she talked about him. Whatever she gave me, I accepted with arms that ached to hold her and a mind that strove to match hers.

She could've been lying, feeding on my concern and admiration, making me into a cruel and calculated performance art project. Or she could've trusted me for whatever reason, sensing my fantasies of saving her. Had I built her up as some sort of magnificent warrior in my mind, when she'd really spent most of her life sitting in her bedroom, carving up her own flesh to satisfy her desire for pain or attention?

Did it matter what I believed?

Elise's gaze turned to her canvas propped on my easel in front of us. We'd been painting together almost every night in my apartment, me on the coffee table and her on the easel atop the tarp I'd spread over the living room floor. Like in the school's paint lab, she created a new layer each night, another woman agape in ecstasy or agony trying to speak to us as Elise smothered her with gesso and started again. Sometimes, when she wasn't looking, I would brush my fingers over the thickening edge of the canvas and test the sticky bounce of those never-ending layers.

"I've only told one other person and she kept trying to prove it," she said, eyes fixed on the woman in her painting. What had in its initial layers looked like a version of

Elise shifted now, the dark, thick brows thinner and lighter, the strong lines of her nose and chin softening the longer I stared. Thin lips parted in a stingy smudge, and I wondered if this newest image was an ex-girlfriend instead, perhaps the one she was talking about now.

"She wanted to confront him and save me," Elise continued. "She wanted to hide in my closet—I don't know what she thought she was going to do, what she thought I hadn't already done. He never came when she was there, of course, so she eventually lost interest, I guess. Called me crazy, treated me like I was a tease or something. I'm not ashamed, Shauna. I'm not hiding what he's done to me, but I'm not telling just anybody either."

I set Elise's knife down on the coffee table and pulled her hand into mine. I savored the fact that I had held her knife, this thing that facilitated the damage she equally returned. Our DNA entwined on the handle, the monster's on the blade. Though I couldn't see it, scrubbed away as it was, the blood he left behind was satisfaction, proof.

"If you can't kill him…how can you hide from him?" I prompted, squeezing my fingers around her palm. "I mean, how can you hide forever?"

Elise pulled her hand from mine. "It wouldn't be forever. He's getting older, and I think weaker too. Whatever he is, he's aging, so he has to die like the rest of us. Twenty years, maybe? I don't know if I can keep fighting him off as I get older and weaker myself, but I can hide for those years. I can wait until he dies." She grabbed the knife from the coffee table and turned it over in her palm. "That night we met, I had a good feeling about you, Shauna—I just knew. Do you trust me? Can I trust you?"

"Yes, of course."

Gripping the knife in her right hand, she pressed the blade's tip next to the scar on her left forearm and, without hesitation, dug in, a hiss escaping through her teeth as a bead of blood surfaced. She dragged the tip all the way around the dark pink line that split her arm from elbow to wrist, outlining the scar in her escaping blood. I gasped. I was as fascinated as I was shocked, not only by the act but by her resolve and how she managed to hold her arm out away from the couch so that her blood collected on the tarp under our feet.

"Elise…What the fuck?"

I jumped to my feet, primed to grab paper towels, antiseptic, Band-Aids—whatever was closest that could stanch the bleeding—but she simply said "no" and "look," directing my gaze to her painting. What had once been a small gap between thin lips widened as we watched, the painted woman's mouth unclenching in a split-jawed scream. Dark irises rolled upwards, leaving only the whites of her eyes as if frozen in climax. Elise's blood dripped quickly, pooling on the tarp and collecting into one bright red mass that crawled away from her and towards the easel.

We watched this red animal, no bigger than my hand, shift and lurch its way up the wooden structure and onto the canvas itself, the painted woman's lips quivering first in anticipation, then rapture as she pulled the blood creature into the chasm of her mouth. The woman swallowed it all with a slurp, returning to her previous pursed-lip pose only after Elise's bleeding had slowed.

"Elise," I gasped again, once I was able to tear my gaze from the painting. She still held her injured arm out, her other hand cupping a small palmful of blood under her wrist. I dashed to the kitchen and returned with a roll of paper towels and hydrogen peroxide.

"I'm okay," she said, dabbing a wad of paper towels along her wound. The ribbon of scar tissue rose shiny and textured against the fresh blood that stained her skin. "You have to trust me, okay? This is working."

"What— What the fuck? What are you doing?"

"This is how I hide. Every few days, I cut myself open and release part of myself into this painting. She's me, but he won't know because every layer I paint is me changing, transforming into something he won't recognize. He's never seen it because I don't keep it at home. Soon, all of me will be in that painting and the me he knows will be gone. He won't be able to touch me."

I looked at the painting. A woman made of paint and blood to save the flesh I loved to touch, to kiss. Every layer a piece of her body as well as a disguise. The painted woman's eyes were heavy-lidded now, as though nodding off after a particularly decadent meal.

"Elise, what I just saw…this is a lot of blood. How long do you have to keep doing this? You're going to end up killing yourself."

She wetted a fresh paper towel with hydrogen peroxide and wiped it down the length of her forearm, all around her scar. I watched as the cut she had made—what should've been a gaping oval of flesh ready to separate itself from the rest of her arm—was erased by the paper towel, not even the whisper of flesh knitting back together at an inhuman speed, not a single scratch or scab to mark what she had done.

"So you drain your blood into that painting, but what happens to the rest of your body? How do you even know this is going to work?"

"I asked you to trust me."

I stood up and went to the easel. Trust. After a lifetime of fighting off an unknowable enemy, Elise trusted wood, cotton, oil paint, and instinct to save her. Not another person. Not me. Under those heavy lids the painted woman stared back at me. Her chest seemed to contract in an inhale. When she exhaled, I felt her warm breath against my own lips, a haze of mineral tang cradling my nostrils.

I'd seen enough to stop asking how any of this was possible, to either believe my own eyes or futilely cling to some semblance of rationality. I wasn't that stubborn, but I was willing to exhaust every possibility.

"So you're just gonna be inside this painting for what, twenty years?" I asked. "This can't be the only solution, Elise. What if you moved in with me? You said he only comes for you when you're alone at night, right? So live with me." I was talking faster than I could think, but living together made more sense than Elise bleeding herself into a painting. It didn't matter that it was too soon in our relationship, that I'd never lived with anyone before—I just wanted her safe, with me. "We can get your stuff now. We'll make it work."

Defeat slumped her face. I'd seen this before, when she talked about the man, but it had never been this heavy. I didn't want to be the cause. "It won't, though," she said.

"We can make sure we're always together at night—that's easy. And if for some reason one of us has to go out of town, we'll go together. We can do it. You're always hearing about these old couples who've never spent a day apart in fifty years. We can—"

"Shauna, please. It sounds romantic now, but it's not, and it won't be in five or ten years. I can't do this anymore. I can't spend my life like this, afraid of when he'll come next, afraid that he'll change his pattern and come for me during the day. And if I get comfortable—what if he gets comfortable? What if he starts coming around when you're with me? What if he attacks you too?"

Then I'll fight with you, I wanted to tell her. *I'll die with you.*

"So if you go into the painting…how will you get out?" I asked. It was still difficult to comprehend, even after what I'd seen. "What happens to you after all that time?"

Elise tossed her used paper towels onto the coffee table and braced her hands on her thighs. When she met my eyes, I saw genuine uncertainty there for the first time. "This is where I have to ask a big favor of you," she said.

The painting needs a week of recuperation before it vomits up the last of Elise.

The bubble on the woman's lips, the wet pop, her eyes closing as the paint cracks under the strain of the dropped-jawed void spilling forth stinking viscera—it's the same as it has been every time. The vomit turns to black tar as it slides down the fireplace to lap at my feet. Pieces of Elise flop onto the floor, chased by placenta-like swollen shapes that may or may not be even more of her.

There's a face. What little I can see is a blurred mask thankfully obscured by a mass of long, blood-wet hair that shines black in the low light. I don't want to look, but I have to know. Has she aged like me? Is she still young? Will this warped face erase the one I remember from twenty years ago? Kneeling on the floor, my legs slipping under me against all the blood and mucus, I try brushing the hair from her forehead, but it sticks. I gently lift a clump from her cheek, but it tugs the skin underneath, pulling up a web of raw flesh, as bright and sticky as freshly-chewed gum. I pat it back down. I have to believe the earth will repair this damage, same as it will birth all the flesh and muscle and bone needed to connect her pieces into one familiar whole.

Next, shoulders, I think. A torso split in two. I recognize the scar below the collarbone, though it's a jumbled mess of indiscernible flesh across her breasts and belly. Her pelvis is similarly mangled, a heap of ambiguous meat and bone encased in mucus, slipping across my floor every time I bend to touch it. These final pieces of Elise look as if they've been vomited up half-digested by some greedy animal that dined in desperation, snarling at shadows with its back against the wall.

Still, despite the revulsion I feel, I treat each piece with care and respect: a kiss on every scar, grace for flavors I don't remember, a jolt of pleasure when my lips stick to her skin. The painting has given me back all of Elise, and I can't fault it for any carelessness due to exhaustion; it has done its duty, just as I am doing mine.

There's nothing more satisfying. It's like tucking her into bed: snuggle in the head, the torso, the pelvis, warm the soil in my hands and spread it over her, imagining all her pieces knitting together under this nutrient-rich blanket. The inside of my house smells of blood and bile, but the air outside is a whirl of sea air, cedar, wet asphalt, juniper on a humid day. I go to bed imagining what it will feel like to unleash the kisses I've been saving all these years. The relief of those kisses returned.

We knew the time was near when she started getting weaker, when the blood loss finally had an effect on her. Elise grew paler, her veins bright pops of blue beneath translucent skin. Each new wound she created—an oval cut around an existing scar as a highlight, a one-upping of each mark the man left on her—no longer magically resealed as I had witnessed before. These cuts she made healed over days and weeks, scabbing up and scarring like regular wounds until the last few simply refused to heal. The red animal of Elise's blood raced to the painting as if it knew it didn't have much time, and the painting quivered with measured delight as if it too knew it needed to savor these last meals.

The last few weeks were busy, even in Elise's fragile state. I stopped going to class, stopped taking phone calls, ignored the half-finished canvases that were supposed to be the launch of my art career. We devoted ourselves to each other, shifting from the distractions of movies and books to memorizing every inch of each other's bodies, to revealing everything about ourselves we could fit into one endless conversation.

She told me about how she left home at seventeen, unable to maintain a relationship with parents who didn't believe her and threatened to institutionalize her every time they spied a new wound or scar. She told me about the jobs she'd held at coffee shops and movie theaters and funeral homes, taking whatever work she could in every new town until she realized she couldn't outrun the man who stalked her. We shared stories of first kisses and drunken fumbles and how we both never knew what to do with the loneliness. We revealed our lies, our humiliations. She admitted she had never been a registered student at my college or anywhere else, instead haunting lecture halls and open studios until she was forced to move on. Under the shadow of the man, what should have been an exhilarating exploratory period in a new relationship bore the weight of duty, with me tasked to preserve this record of her life either to remind her who she'd been when she returned in twenty years, or bear proof that she had existed should she fail to return.

The morning she got the varnish out, my stomach sank.

"Not yet," I sputtered, still dazed from sleep when I found the bottle sitting on the coffee table. Though the cap was still on, the odor intensified as I approached. I usually found the slightly sweet haze comforting, but now, nausea snaked through my gut. "Put it away."

Elise came out of the kitchen wearing my hoodie unzipped over her PJ Harvey t-shirt, the same one she'd worn the night we met. She offered me a mug of coffee, but I refused to take it, stuffing my hands under my armpits as if that would make it all stop.

"You knew, Shauna," she said, setting both mugs on the coffee table. When she tried to touch my arm, I tightened my grip on myself. "This is the only way. I'm ready."

"One more week," I said.

"The painting's done."

The woman stared at us from her perch on the easel. Arms over breasts, head tilted back, eyes closed, repose turned to anticipation—and a mouth I swore was grinning in that moment. I considered taking Elise's hunting knife to the canvas, slashing through paint and fabric until the woman was a blur of muddied colors and no longer a face, no longer a vague and greedy representation of the woman I loved.

"She still looks like you," I said. "You could paint over her a hundred times and he's gonna know. What makes you think he won't find you here?"

"He's never seen the painting. He's never seen you. As long as you keep it…"

My head pounded with the pressure of blood and that acrid-sweet resin odor bullying my nostrils. I snatched the bottle of varnish from the table intending to throw it out the window—then saw it was not the open bottle from my supply, but a new unopened bottle, an expensive brand I'd been coveting. She was making this act, this final day, a ceremony.

"Why me? Why do you trust me? You hardly know me."

"Shauna…"

"Is it because you need me—like *me*—or is it because I'm the one who happened to walk into the paint lab that night?"

Elise approached again, but I stepped back until I hit the wall. When she reached for me, I hurled the bottle of varnish across the room. It hit the bookcase but didn't shatter, instead skidding across the floor with a deep thud that echoed in my throbbing head.

I let her squeeze my shoulders, but I couldn't look at her.

"You've been with me the whole way," she said. "I trust you. Please, we're almost there."

"Move in with me. You've been staying here almost every night and he hasn't touched you. I'll always be here. You'll never be alone."

Her smile was as gentle as her voice and I felt like a child then, struggling under my insurmountable incomprehension and her pity. "I told you. We can't always be in the same room, every minute of every day," she said. "I can't live like this forever. I can't with the what-ifs."

"Why you? Don't you want to know? How can you just accept this?"

"I need this to end, Shauna, even if that means I have to hide in a fucking painting for twenty years. I haven't been able to kill him, so I need to outlive him. It's either this or *he* kills *me*."

I dropped onto the couch and Elise followed. That painting was going to be the center of my home for decades, as lacquered and rich as a mahogany coffin.

"I'm so tired and I'm so scared," she said, resting her head on my shoulder.

"I'm scared too." I pulled her hand into mine, reveling in the warmth of her skin, willing myself to memorize the lines of her palm, the texture of the tiny scars between her fingers rubbing against mine. It wasn't that I thought the man would attack me in an effort to get to Elise, or that I doubted I could protect the painting. I was scared that she wouldn't come back. I was scared that I'd be alone again.

Elise rolled up her jeans to the knee and propped her exposed leg on the coffee table. Her shin still bore an unmarred length of skin, having been one of the last parts of her body to heal before the decline. She reached into her bag and pulled out the hunting knife carefully, as if she was trying to keep it from my view.

"Thank you, Shauna," she said.

It's a foggy early morning two days later when the earth in my backyard finally stirs.

Just enough time to test my patience, make me doubt that I've done everything right, make me regret going along with this when every part of me had screamed that I should've somehow made her run away with me those twenty years ago. *How dramatic*, I think as I watch the dirt rumble, giddy with vindication at my bedroom window, and I'm already imagining how I'll tease her about this theatrical resurrection.

I can't get outside fast enough. It doesn't matter that I'm wearing only a t-shirt and socks, that it's barely forty degrees outside, that my neighbors, despite the fog, might see me with a nude woman rising from her grave. My only regret once I'm out there is that I didn't think to bring a blanket for Elise.

Dry soil sprays up then sinks with the movements of what's underneath, a cascade of crumbs fleeing from fingers as they break the seal. Pale hands surface, dusted brown with earth and cobwebbed with tiny roots, reaching at opposite sides as if searching for armrests to lift out of a chair. I stand back, torn between the urge to yank her out myself and the desire to drink in the second most unreal thing I've ever witnessed.

Besides, I could hurt her, break all we sacrificed to build, if I interfere. This is a birth after all, both savage and delicate in untrained hands.

Toes come next, feet kicking against her confines, flinging more loose dirt like a swimmer splashing through water. Her hands find and grip packed earth and she starts to pull herself up, the top of her head emerging, cascades of dirt and pebbles and dead leaves falling away as her head then neck then shoulders surface. Her long dark hair, studded with the same detritus, hangs wet over her face, and I'm afraid she can't see me, she can't breathe.

"Elise!" I yell, but she doesn't respond.

As I run to her, the rest of her body rises from the hole I dug: a sunken chest, a ladder of ribs leading down to a concave stomach, narrow hips, pelvis and thighs dressed in a thick smear of wet earth dripping down spindly legs. Did she waste away in that painting? Did I do something wrong? But, through the thinning fog I see the dark pink crescent scar below her collarbone, the slashes on her arms and legs, a glimpse of the shiny ridge of scar tissue along her neck. Every mark is a bright beacon, a reassurance despite the doubts collecting in my mind.

Cedar, sea air, wet asphalt, juniper—just like when I buried all those pieces the painting vomited up. It's the scent that's been burned into my memory for the last twenty years, and that is enough.

She stands outside her grave now, hair sucked into her mouth, her chest heaving in a gasp of brown mist. Up close, I inhale a sour stench like wizened skin under a bandage. Perhaps my memories were wrong, romanticized— I've spent two decades in love with an image, after all— but I can't allow my face to reveal my disappointment. I've withered out of youth myself, and everything hinges on her reaction to me.

I reach through the mist, but stop just short of touching her. I should be pulling her to my chest, pushing the hair from her face, warming her with my body. Comforting her. Instead, she lifts two big hands and wipes the mess of wet hair from her face.

Heavy lids lift to reveal pale eyes. Long creases mar a broad forehead and drooping cheeks. Thin lips part into a grin.

I know this face because it's as Elise described. I know who it is.

It wasn't as I'd imagined, what I had feared. She didn't bleed the last of herself into that painting, skin and bone and teeth following in a pink and black flow, sucked into a thirsty canvas until all that was left was a puff of cedar-scented smoke and a few dark hairs twined around my fingers. She sliced a long oval around the scar on her leg and we watched that red animal slink up the easel as we had all the other times. We kissed and held each other and kept kissing. I kept her as close as I could, braced for her to slip into the ether when I should have been enjoying the taste of her mouth, the soft heat of her skin, the brush of peach fuzz against my lips. We both cried, then laughed about how we'd neglected to plan a last night out, a last meal, one last time in the shower as she gripped fistfuls of my dark hair in her hands. There were instructions for what I was to do in twenty years, then plans for our reunion. We fell asleep in each other's arms as she told me what she hoped to see, and I teased her about all the things I'd have to teach her when she awoke to a changed world.

Elise's voice was fresh in my ears as I dozed off, her warm touch slacking against my own as she too gave in to sleep. When I woke up later that night, she was simply gone.

There was no point, but I looked in every room and closet of my apartment. I searched my building and walked the surrounding blocks. I stood outside her building and squinted into the dark squares of her windows, trying to discern any movement. It was only when I was too cold and too tired and too hungry that I went home and cried.

With narrowed eyes, the painting watched me as she always had. Was Elise really in there, all of her? Head slightly tilted back, maybe on the verge of a laugh this time instead of sleep. Hair snaked to her hips, arms obscuring her breasts. A mouth I knew by heart. Would there come a day when I could objectively look at this painting and not see Elise? She begged for a knife slash through that painted face, the time to start again, but it was too late now.

I cleared off the coffee table and laid the canvas flat. I grabbed the bottle of fancy new varnish from the floor and a large foam brush from my tackle box. I would do this right, make it the ceremony she wanted.

It felt good pouring the thick, clear liquid onto the painting, satisfying to watch it pool on the woman's face and imagine it suffocating that smugly-secretive hint of a smile. I worked horizontally, using the foam brush to spread the varnish in long unbroken strokes from one end to the other. I was careful and neat as I'd always been as a painter. As I went over the canvas again, smoothing out my brush strokes, it occurred to me that this was why Elise chose me, not because she loved me but the assurance that I would do everything she asked as precisely as possible.

Treacly fumes rose around me, cradling my temples and blurring my vision as I sat back to admire my work. If she was right, Elise was now fully in there, not just sealed under my layer of glossy glass, but in every brushstroke, swirled into every drop of paint spread thick and thin and cured, every mark of her pencil, every fiber of that canvas. Was she behind those eyes rolled up beneath heavy lids, watching me or fighting sleep? Had she surveyed me with approval as I closed the tomb? Would I sense a response if I said her name?

The painting needed to remain undisturbed as the varnish dried, but I couldn't bear to leave her there alone in the dark. I turned on the TV to keep myself awake, but it was a failed distraction. I longed to fall asleep right where I was and wake up decades later to Elise's kiss on my forehead, her toothy grin as she filled me in on all I had missed. I wanted to be the one sealed into that painting, watching her protect and love and wait for me.

When I finally dragged myself to bed, I found a large manila envelope under my pillow. Elise had closed her bank account and left the cash for me along with a key to her apartment and instructions to sell or give away her belongings. In the morning light, I found her hunting knife and her PJ Harvey t-shirt neatly folded on the floor next to her side of the bed.

Maybe she had become a wisp of smoke dissolved into the ether. Maybe I could breathe her in and she could live in me.

No, it was just as she'd said. Elise had disappeared into that canvas as abruptly as she'd appeared in the paint lab, her physical body slipping out of my life same as she'd slipped in.

He shakes off the atrophy with the dirt and lunges towards me, long legs carrying him so fast I barely make it back into the house. A rope of his long hair catches in the door as I lock it, but he tears free in seconds, showing no regard for pain or the flesh left behind. He makes no sounds other than the slap of his hands against my windows as he follows me from outside the house. Greasy handprints and endless exhales of earth-filled lungs coat the glass as I race to find a safe space to think, to hide, to figure out what went wrong.

That fucking grin.

Hungry, waiting, baring yellowed teeth at me every time I walked by that painting, cheeks flushing with lust or amusement or ridicule when I put on a dress that made me feel sexy, when I did a silly little dance that was supposed to be for her. He was the one smiling back at me all these years, not Elise.

I intend to barricade myself in the bedroom, call the police—I don't fucking know what I'll tell them—but instead I stop in the living room, in front of the painting. This woman Elise created from endless layers of herself has birthed a monster, and she still wears that tired hint of a smile like an exhausted new mother.

Fucking liar. He tricked me. He tricked us.

The stench of congealed blood and bile lingers in the air. I stare at that painted mouth, those vomit-burnt lips so pale and cracked now, and I wait for her to tell me she feels better now that she's gotten it all out. *Him* out. Has Elise been trapped inside this painting with her attacker the whole time? Was she subdued behind him as he gazed at me with those eyes, grinned at me with lips I thought I knew? What did he do to her in there and why didn't I know?

"I'm sorry," I croak. "What do I do?"

I raise a fist, imagine punching that canvas, turning fabric and wood to pulp until I can plunge my hands all the way in and pull those pieces of Elise out.

"Elise? Fuck, are you in there?"

The painted woman's heavy lids lift. A spark lights up darkened irises, lips gathering to cradle a bubble about to pop. The paint along her jaw cracks, hot orange blistering outward from the bubble, splitting her mouth in a scream.

The man slaps his big hands against the window to the left of the fireplace. All of him is out there, united as if nothing ever happened—I buried two hands, two feet, two arms, two legs, a head, a pelvis, a torso—but I see now the painting isn't empty. Elise is still in there, screaming for me, trying to force herself out in a painted jaw moving up and down, a bare chest seizing, its eyes bulging as the painting dry heaves. Pupils swing to my left, a desperate warning as the man pounds the glass, grinning at me, shaking the house.

He gets in no matter what. I've moved so many times—he finds me every time. It's always the same. I can't stop him, but I can fight back.

I know him because he's as Elise described, as I imagined, the figure I've searched crowds and closets for all these years. She endured, fought, then made a plan that both worked and didn't. Two minutes with him pursuing me and I'm shaking, raw, unable to think straight. I could never survive days, weeks, months, years of this. Elise is the strongest person I've ever known.

I grab the hunting knife from the mantle and hold the blade against my extended forearm. When Elise painted this portrait, she intended to put only herself into it, but maybe I'm in there too. Those layers were open, wet, and clutching for anything and everything the moment I walked into that paint lab; the pigment suckled at every flake of skin, every loose hair swirling in the air. Saliva, dandruff, tears—Elise spent many nights painting in my apartment, every fresh layer a magnet for my DNA. I was the last person to touch that painting, sealing more of myself in with the varnish.

When I take the knife to my flesh, the pain is worse than I imagined, much more than Elise ever let on. The tip of the blade breaks the tender underside of my arm after three hesitant attempts, blood slow to surface as if my own biology is resisting. I'm sweating, shaking, vision blurred with tears. I know this is foolish, a long shot, but what other choice do I have? Suffer this relentless attacker while

I rush to paint my own self-portrait, all the while trying to meet someone I can trust enough to usher the last of me into that image? That is a whole other life, not the one I spent the bulk of my own imagining and planning for. If Elise is still in there, I'd rather be with her—whatever he left of her, no matter how battered and broken she may be—than out here, alone except for *him*.

As the blood flows down the length of my forearm, pooling in a slow drip at my elbow, the painted woman's mouth drops open in a larger O, her eyes rolling upward in trembling anticipation. Pustules of paint crackle and pop, but she's not releasing—she's inhaling, lips rooting for the raw human viscera she craves.

Once enough of my blood collects into a mass the size of my hand, it starts feeling along the floor, instinctively drawn to the one who craves it. The red animal hauls itself up onto the hearth, climbs each brick of the fireplace, lurches onto the polished mantle. When it reaches the spot where Elise's hunting knife was displayed, the painted woman makes a wet sucking noise and the canvas seems to buck from the wall, straining towards my blood. Her mouth gapes, revealing clean white teeth. My blood quickens up the wall and eagerly hauls itself into her painted jaws.

Eyelids heavy again, she sighs. Elise sighs. But her mouth stays open, the tip of her tongue teasing teeth now stained red.

And then she does something she's never done before. The painting says my name.

Not out loud, but her lips form the shapes of my letters, the pucker of the *S*, the spread of the *N*, the drift of the last *A*.

Shauna…

I don't wait to see if my wound instantly heals like Elise's did. This time, I plunge the knife into my upper arm with no hesitation. The man pounds on the window again, pale eyes huge and glassy as if drunk on the anticipation of my blood on his hands. I could never cut him for every cut he gave me—not like Elise—but I can join her, and I can believe from the wear I see on him, the papery skin and bone-clung flesh, that he will not survive should he attempt to drain himself into this painting with us again.

Shauna…

Again and again, I cut myself open until the sharp pain dulls to a warm, not unpleasant burn, and the edges of my vision go fuzzy. I feel myself falling back, held in a palm of damp air, a tunnel that points me directly to her. To my Elise. Every new red animal I make grows bigger and stronger, crawling to shuffling to striding into Elise's waiting mouth. She slurps and bloats and my eyes are so heavy and I am so warm, so held. Is this what she felt that last night, as I slept in ignorance on the couch? I remember finding her shirt and knife next to my bed. Who will find what's left of me? Who will seal me into this lacquered coffin?

I don't care. Not when the scents of cedar and rain-wet asphalt bloom around me. Not when I feel her fold her body—intact, exactly as I remember—around mine, the satiny ridges of her scars sliding hot and alive against my skin. Her long dark hair in my mouth as she kisses me. As she wants me, still. The distant familiarity of sinking into warm liquid, of making a whole new animal, as her lips trace every one of my fresh, already-forming scars.

ABOUT THE AUTHORS

PATRICK BARB is an author of weird, dark, and horrifying tales, currently living (and trying not to freeze to death) in Saint Paul, Minnesota. He is the author of the novellas *Gargantuana's Ghost* (Grey Matter Press), *Turn* (Alien Buddha Press), and *The Nut House* (serialized in Cosmic Horror Monthly, collected edition from Brigids Gate Press in late 2024), as well as the novelette *Helicopter Parenting in the Age of Drone Warfare* (Spooky House Press), the forthcoming dark fiction collection *Pre-Approved for Haunting* (Keylight Books / Turner Publishing, September 2023), and the forthcoming novel *Abducted* (Dark Matter INK, Fall 2024). He is an Active Member of the HWA and a Full Member of the SFWA. Visit him at patrickbarb.com.

J.A.W. McCARTHY is the Bram Stoker Award and Shirley Jackson Award nominated author of *Sometimes We're Cruel and Other Stories* (Cemetery Gates Media, 2021) and *Sleep Alone* (Off Limits Press, 2023). Her short fiction has appeared in numerous publications, including *Vastarien*, *PseudoPod*, *LampLight*, *Apparition Lit*, *Tales to Terrify*, and *The Best Horror of the Year Vol 13* (ed. Ellen Datlow). She is Thai American and lives with her husband and assistant cats in the Pacific Northwest. You can call her Jen on Twitter @JAWMcCarthy, and find out more at www.jawmccarthy.com.

ABOUT THE ARTISTS

RYAN MILLS is an avid reader, illustrator and cover artist of horror and thriller novels, including the Juniper Trilogy by Ross Jeffery, the My Dark Library series of novellas curated by Sadie Hartmann, and most works by Tyler Jones. You can see more of his work on Twitter @ryanm642, or at his website, ryanmills.art.

EVANGELINE GALLAGHER is an award-winning illustrator from Baltimore, Maryland. They received their BFA in Illustration from the Maryland Institute College of Art in 2018. When they aren't drawing they're probably hanging out with their dog, Charlie, or losing at a board game. They possess the speed and enthusiasm of 10,000 illustrators.

ACKNOWLEDGMENTS

PATRICK BARB – Thanks to Gemma Files and my fellow students in her "Write What You Fear" course. You all were there as this project was birthed in fright.

Thanks also to Alex Ebenstein for helping this beast grow and meet its monstrous potential.

J.A.W. McCARTHY – This is a selfish story, one I started without the usual eye towards publication. That people are reading this visceral indulgence of blood, saliva, and loose body parts is both intimidating and gratifying. Thanks for sticking with me.

Thanks to Alexis DuBon, Shelley Lavigne, and Jacob Steven Mohr for their early reading, suggestions, and push to emphasize the beauty in the gross. Extra thanks to Jacob for the Latin advice.

Much gratitude to my fellow Nervous Drivers, who not only patiently listened but encouraged my vomiting painting obsession. Their enthusiasm and support of my puke-y musings reminds me that I can't do this alone.

As always, love and gratitude to my family.

And thank you to Dread Stone Press and Alex Ebenstein for editing and indulging everything I wanted to say about art, school, devotion, and love.

CONTENT WARNINGS

These stories are works of horror fiction which contain dark content that may be triggering to some individuals. In addition to instances and implications of graphic violence and death throughout, there are instances of blood, gore, stalking, stabbing, cutting, self-harm, scars, and codependency in "Imago Expulsio." Please read with caution.

TENEBROUS PRESS

aims to drag the malleable Horror genre into newer, Weirder territory with stories that are incisive, provocative, intelligent and terrifying; delivered by voices diverse and unsung.

FIND OUT MORE:
www.tenebrouspress.com
Social Media @TenebrousPress

NEW WEIRD HORROR